Harry Harrison was born in Stamford, Connecticut, grew up in New York City and, promptly on his eighteenth birthday, was drafted into the United States Army. Returning to civilian life some years later, he pursued careers as an artist, art director and editor until, one day, he found himself following a new occupation as a free-lance writer. Since then he has lived with his family in more than twenty-seven countries including Mexico, England, Italy and Denmark. The Harrisons now live in Ireland.

By the same author

HARRY HARRISON

You Can Be The Stainless Steel Rat

An Interactive Game Book

Illustrated by Dave McKean

GRAFTON BOOKS
A Division of the Collins Publishing Group

LONDON GLASGOW
TORONTO SYDNEY AUCKLAND

Grafton Books
A Division of the Collins Publishing Group
8 Grafton Street, London W1X 3LA

Published by Grafton Books 1985
Reprinted 1987

Copyright © Harry Harrison 1985

ISBN 0-586-06359-5

Printed and bound in Great Britain by
Collins, Glasgow

Set in Plantin

You Can Be
The
Stainless Steel
Rat

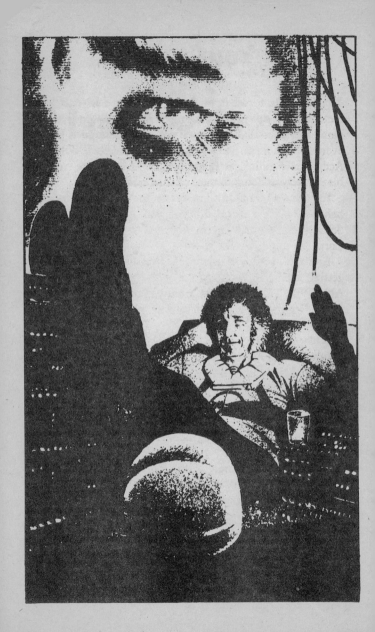

WELCOME ABOARD

That's it, step forward, don't be shy. I can't say that we've met before – this organization gets bigger all the time. My name is James diGriz, sometimes called Slippery Jim, or even the Stainless Steel Rat, or occasionally Il Titano di Accaio, or Ratinox, or if you haven't heard of me what the blazes are you doing in the Special Corps?!

Excuse me, shouldn't lost my temper with new recruits, heh-heh. Have a drink, I'll join you – what? – you don't drink reconstituted Jovian Lynxbat sweat? What *is* the Corps coming to . . .?

Anyway, you're a strapping recruit. Are the recruits getting younger – or am I getting older – DON'T ANSWER THAT! Let us kindly stick with the matter in hand. Which is . . . I have a note here somewhere, yes, here it is.

Welcome to the Special Corps, oh new recruit. You hold in your hand your first assignment as a Trainee Field Agent, this assignment being cunningly designed as a paperback, role-playing book – *which it is not!* I cannot stress that fact too firmly. What appears to be paper is really indestructible impervium – don't try to tear a page or it will slice your fingers to ribbons.

You have just failed your first test, oh potential Full Field Agent who is now acting like a dumb recruit. You tore the page, didn't you? From now on you will obey orders instantly without thinking. By reflex. Because you are in the Corps now –

TURN TO 30 NOW!!!

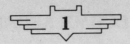

If you said Sulphuric Acid score 578 points and go at once to **229**. But, hark – it speaks!

'One last chance, dumb squishy one. What important event occurred in 1066 A.D., Old Dirt Time, which was a damn long time ago?'

Got it? Turn to **298**.

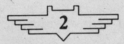

Of course I know that you are tired, so a small rest is in order. Better now? Push on up the hill to the path. This should lead back to Crapper's Castle – but you will be a little more careful this time. Just two invisibility charges left in the belt, you know. Hsst! Thrashings and crunchings from around the bend. If you have had enough bashing about for a bit you can turn off the path and creep stealthily away to **4**. If, however, you want to see what is happening you can peep around the bend at **216**.

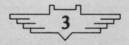

Yes, the beach is closer. You land safely. Oh, well, perhaps my fears were all to naught. Yes, laugh, I deserve that. But what is that that rustles in the bushes? To discover the answer turn to **218**.

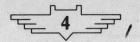

4

That is one difficulty avoided. But I think I hear another. Isn't that a moaning from the bushes over there? Could be a trap of some kind – or it could be someone in desperate need. You want to investigate? You do have the makings of a field agent after all! Turn slowly and carefully to **134**.

5

Don't hang your head in shame. So you missed, so what? So you missed two in a row. So what? So he is neck and neck with you and you have to hit this next one or you lose. So don't think about it. Draw and fire and heads you go to **9**, tails to **286**. And good luck . . .

6

'Stop!' the guard commands in a growly voice. '**Who goes there?**'

'Me,' you respond with very little imagination.

'**Advance Me and give the password.**'

You move forward slowly and attempt a ruse.

'**The password is antidisestablishmentarianism.**'

It's a good ruse – but not good enough. Swinging his club the guard jumps forward shouting, '**You're a spy – that's yesterday's password!**'

If you step aside to dodge the blow go to **232**. Or if you counter his blow with your sword go to **76**.

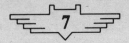

7

Rarely in life do we get a second chance. You just got a second chance. Go back to **94** and think again.

8

The empty desert has now given way to ancient, brooding ruins, a city that had been dead for millennia, deserted and decaying while the ancestors of mankind were still swinging from trees and scratching fleas . You think about this, but not too deeply, because you're still on the prof's trail through the jumbled stones. But – look!

The footsteps end in a hole in the ground! The sand has caved in and the professor has gone! What can have happened to him? You go close and read the sign carved into an immense block of stone beside the hole.

WARNING! SAND IS DANGEROUS HERE AND THERE HAVE BEEN CAVE-INS AND PEOPLE LOST IN THE CAVERNS BELOW. YOU COULD BE NEXT.

What's that crunching sound? Watch out – you *are* next! You scrabble away but are too late. The ground falls away and you drop into **253**.

9

You've done it! Bullseye number three and you are the winner. Robbing Good, poor loser he, throws his bow on to the ground and jumps up and down on it. Oh well, let him have his tantrum. You smile and watch and when he is done you tell him to pay up. He must do you the favour, the promised favour.

'Yeah, yeah, I know, the favour. I even know what it is.'

He knows what favour you want? Goodness, how can he know that? To discover what he knows flip now to 23.

Oh what pain! He is almost in your grasp but you must let him escape. If you were shot dead you would not be able to go after him again; very wise thinking. You wait until he has gone through the turret door and hurry after him to 148.

Money. Gold coins. Hurray! Shake them out and fondle their still warm bulk in your hand. Great. Now what are you going to do with them?

Buy information of course, very wise. Put a sign up on the town bulletin board offering a reward of three gold coins for any information leading to the apprehension of one mad scientist, name of Prof. Geisteskrank. Any person or persons who have information of his whereabouts to meet you at dawn by the gallows just outside of town. A gruesome venue, but one that should be easy to find. That will do it all right – you should get a lead or two that way. You should also get every nutcase and thug on the planet there to bash you on the head. Oh, you've thought of that as well? How about letting an old Stainless Steel Rat in on the secret?

Very wise. You will bury the gold and not say where it is hidden until you have found the prof. It's a good plan – if you can get your informant to go along with it. Where are you going to bury the coins? You won't tell *me*? Well, you are probably right. I'll find out in any case, since I am watching this adventure through your eyes. I'll control my impatience until we reach **140**.

That did it all right. Someone's coming through the woods. Pulling you out, saving your life, you've lost your staff – but you are saved.

Or are you? Do you recognize that great build and wild laughter? I thought you might. It's Betsy Booster – and she has caught you again.

So, kicking and screaming you are dragged once more to **65**. But you are in luck – Arbuthnot is there as well. *This* time you should know what to do!

You have wisely decided to shoot the filthy thing – and I don't blame you! With careful motions you slot an arrow to the string . . . draw back the bow –

It attacks! You let fly! Your arrow zings out and to discover what has happened you zing to **88**.

That was very smart thinking. You never know who – or what – you can trust on this prison planet. Things are not nice here. Go back the way you came and . . . you heard a rustling? Someone in the woods there! A dim shape emerging . . . it is surely a shape that you recognize – indeed! It is that girl again. I think she likes you, going to all that trouble to find you. You want to meet her? Well, if you insist – turn to **99**.

This is hard work. The big orange fruit are each about the size of a grapefruit, only the wrong colour of course. They are high in the trees and you have to climb up to get them. Each one is attached by a tough stem that will not break. You try cutting one off with your sword – and it works fine.

Except the fruit plunges to the ground and explodes with a juicy splosh. Be more careful next time. Hold the stem, then cut it – that's it. Then climb carefully down and place the fruit on the ground. And climb the tree for more.

Time passes slowly until you have all that you can carry on the ground. With a bit of vine you tie all their stems together, get the orange bundle over your shoulder – and stagger fruitily to **113**.

A boring half an hour has passed and no one has emerged from the tavern. You are getting thirsty and are intrigued by the sounds of joyous revelry from inside. Better turn to **139**.

When you've seen one black tunnel you've seen them all. Good thing that you don't have claustrophobia – don't curse at me that way! I'm sorry I said it, I take it back. So cool and restful here in the endless night . . .

You run when you see the light ahead. What can be waiting for you? The only way that you will find out is by turning to 115.

Yes, I would sweat too in the circumstances. Not much you can do with four uglies carrying you, is there? My, such language. In the kitchen – look at the size of that black pot on the fire! Looks like they are going to shell you, I mean pluck you, I mean *undress* you, before they throw you into the boiling water. You are hurled to the ground and two thugs pull at your boots.

I was hoping you would think of that. Invisibility. Press the buckle and turn to 87.

Nothing to fear here. A nice stroll down this softly lit tunnel. Yes, the carvings on the wall do seem a bit repulsive with those monsters eating other monsters. Eyes front! Best not to dwell on their sinister horror . . .

Aha – the tunnel widens – then ends. There's one set of steps leading down, labelled STAR BEAST HERE. And more steps leading up with a sign saying SAFE WAY OUT. You'd better decide. Are they lying – or truthful? Go up to 124, or down to 49.

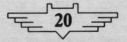

Tummy full? Good. I don't know if you want any advice – but I would go to 97 and see if the old man has come back – and ask him the way.

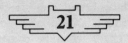

You get exactly what you deserve trusting a figure as repellent as Hairy Harry the Killer Cannibal. As soon as you are out of sight of the others he throws you to the ground and sinks his fangs into your throat. You whisper where the coins are buried – hoping that his greed will overpower his appetite.

It does! He rushes away and you sink into the pit of despair. As well you might. Trapped forever on this loathsome planet. Maybe. You look up when you hear that, don't you? Maybe. Now it can be told. I've kept this secret for last. Listen to me and stop feeling sorry for yourself for one moment. There is one thing I haven't told you about yet. I was saving it for the right moment and this looks like the moment. While you were under hypnosis – you didn't know we had you hypnotized did you? The Special Corps does not reveal all its secrets! Anyway, while you were hypnotized, we planted a miniature time machine in the joint of your right index finger. All you have to do is crack your knuckle to energize it. That's it, don't feel foolish, pull hard on your finger. As soon as it goes crack you will go to **80**.

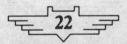

Your plan has been accepted – nay, not only accepted but cheered by your followers. All of them have lost dear friends to the voracious appetite of Hairy Harry the Killer Cannibal. They wish to end his vile gastronomic career. All of them are also hardened criminals – or they wouldn't be here, would they? They welcome the chance to turn the tables on Hairy Harry – dining tables, of course – and loot his castle as well. Giving you a chance to grab the evil Professor and finish his case.

A simple plan and it should be a good one. Sluj the Slaver roars with anger when he comes to – but he is chained with the other slaves and is happily beaten into submission by his former beatees. You are chained too, at the front, while Arbuthnot leads the way in the guise of a slavemaster. Up the hill to Crapper's Castle. To get there yourself turn to **34**.

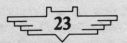

'How do I know what favour you want?' he asks. 'I know because everyone in the jungle knows that Sadie the Sadistic sent you to the Juicy Jungle to get her the Jewel of the Jungle. I also know that you are as good as dead, or deader, if you don't get some advice on how to grab the jewel. The only one who knows how that can be done lies at the end of yonder trail and yonder trail begins at **260**. I can tell you no more or I risk death. Begone varlet, for I wish to see no more of you.'

So you leave, careful not to turn your back on this dirty ruffian, down the trail to **260**.

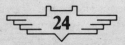

What a sight! Blue sky above, red-stained yellow sand below. Are the red stains blood? I couldn't say, best not to think about it. Listen to the roar of the crowd. I wonder what they are so excited about? Oh, yes, I see now, a great lion has just entered the arena through a little door. It roars and yawns, looks about – and sees you. It seems to be smiling. And, yes, it is coming this way. You raise the feather, not really the best weapon.

It stands before you and roars again, its breath washes over you in a fetid wave, it approaches . . .

If you feel that tickling it with the feather will make it laugh and not eat you, why then go to **332**.

If jumping aside when it leaps seems preferable, go to **302**.

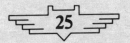

Why does the old dear look so frightened and shy away from you? Have you bathed lately? No, that is not the reason, it is because this is a world of violence and everyone is afraid of everyone else. Not a very profound observation, but you are probably right. So what do you do? Play the role like everyone else and twist granny's arm so she'll tell you where to find Prof. Geisteskrank? Or do you want to bribe her with a small coin?

A bribe will get you to **90**, while a twist of the arm and a shrill scream will land you on **167**.

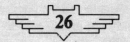

Yes, a gold coin does seem dear for a ride in this crummy boat. But look at the alternative – no, don't look at the shore! You have averted your eyes from the evil boatman and he is attacking, trying to steal your money. Ouch, that must have hurt – NO! – don't back away.

Splash. Yes indeed, you have fallen into the river in **205**.

So you missed. You can't win them all. Grit your teeth, take careful aim and let fly – to **84** with heads or **289** with tails.

Unhappily another fight has been lost. You are bound and thrown on the floor in Crapper's Castle. Hark, someone is coming. They drag you to your feet and down the hall to **121**.

That hurt, I know. Believe me I really feel sorry for you, even though I feel nothing myself. Look, we all make mistakes. I might even have done the same thing. Very few people in this galaxy are immune to my sleep gas bombs. In fact that thug is the only one I have ever met.

Just wait until the door is opened again. This time you will have to use the smokebomb that will take you inexorably to **64**.

Now that's more like it. Should you accept this assignment, and you have absolutely no choice in the matter anyway, you will be transmitted by the newly invented, and still not reliable, matter transmitter to the planet Skraldespand. Your task will be a simple one. You will search for and find a certain scientist by the name of Prof Geisteskrank. When you find him just shake his hand, while pressing the button on this pocket matter-transmitter at the same time. You will both return here and that is that.

Questions? What do you mean you have questions? No, this is not kidnapping. You might call it a matter of protective custody. It seems that the good professor, besides being as nutty as a bag of cashews, has invented a weapon of such awful destruction that I shiver thinking about it. You better shiver too – THAT IS AN ORDER! – good, because if you don't complete this assignment it may mean the end of the universe as we know it. Or rather as I know it because I know it a lot better than you do, recruit. So get out there and win! The die is cast, the matter transmitter turned on, and you are whisked instantly to **42**.

TURN AT ONCE TO 42!

If you answered 'an elephant that sticks to the roof of your mouth' you have scored 25 points more. You jump as there is a roar of flame and this booms out: **'An easy one. Now here is one that will have you on the ropes. What is the Lamb Shift?'** Laughing at the simplicity of the answer, you turn to **292**.

He is suspicious all right – but Arbuthnot offers him a big bribe. They slip into the guardhouse for the bribery and you are the only one who hears the loud thud. Arbuthnot's idea of a bribe saves a lot of money. This happy business over with, you proceed instantly to **118**.

33

What's that? Louder – I can't hear you if you keep putting your head under the mud like that. You're still sinking? Pushing with the staff isn't doing any good.

You'd better start screaming then: scream all the way to **12**.

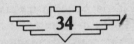

34

Your happy band of slaves wends its way to the castle gate. They wipe the smirks from their faces and try to look enslaved as they approach the guards at the gate. Sluj starts to shout a warning but is dropped by Arbuthnot's ready club. The sadistic guards roar with laughter at this and you try a sick smile yourself. The slaver enslaved, they really like that.

All except the sergeant of the guard. He is so tough that he has sewed his stripes to his *bare skin* and that is pretty tough indeed. Something doesn't smell right to him – though all you can smell is odour du unwashed-slave. He strides forward. You craftily take out your APB, or coin as you insist on calling it, and give it a quick toss. If it comes up heads, he voices his suspicions and you turn to **32**. If he opens the gate then tails tells you to go to **118**.

35

You must enjoy being knocked on the head – because the prof was hiding outside the door, banged you into unconsciousness – and has escaped. Pull yourself to your feet and stagger groggily after him to **197**.

36

You must be joking! Get to **120** at once!

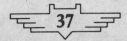

37

Your respite is shortlived, as it says in the good book. Hairy Harry cannot bear the sight of your plump limbs being dragged away. 'No!' he bellows. 'Appetite before science! To the kitchen with him!' Turn to **18**.

38

'Kind sir,' the lad says, 'It is nice to see you are interested in my fate – but nothing can be done. I was a prisoner of Sluj the Slaver – and he is such a terrible man. He beat me when I did not walk fast enough to keep up with the other slaves, then he broke my leg and left me here to die. But perhaps it is better to die here than in Crapper's Castle because that is where he was bringing us.'

You are touched by the suffering boy's story so you whip out your minimedic and press it to his broken leg. Wow! These robot devices work fast. Needles inject him instantly with antibiotics and painkillers, two flexible arms

grip his leg and twist – the fracture is quickly reduced –
while a nozzle ejects some instantly hardening casting
material. The leg is mended. The lad stares in amazement,
then tears of joy flood from his eyes as he kisses your hand
over and over until it is coated with saliva.

'You are my saviour, smack-smack. If only you could
save the others from slavery your name would ring down
through the ages.'

Your head is turned by this flattery – and you want to go
wash your hand as well – so you start back up the path and
trudge to **216**.

The hall winds away through the repellent palace, bones
everywhere. Hungry Harry sure was hungry. Was that the
slam of a door ahead? Run on. Yes, there it is – and
scarcely breaking pace you bash the door down and leap
through – club ready. There he is, your quarry, the mad
professor. After him! He darts through another door and
you follow. He is escaping across the castle roof – after
having jumped an airshaft. If that old nutter can do it – so
can you. Gather your strength and leap instantly to **255**.

Well, you can't win them all. You have missed the tree
completely while his arrow thunks into the very heart of
the bullseye. Ignore his leer of victory. Nock up again,
raise and fire. Heads you go to **254**, tails to **284**.

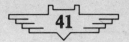

41

Sadie thinks about your request and nods. **'You are right, stranger. Those mugs will eat you alive for breakfast.'** She snaps out orders and a chest is quickly carried up. She throws it open and points inside.

'I have a few extra weapons – but not many. Help yourself to one of these – then split because being so generous goes against my nature.'

If you take the bow and arrows, nip off to **315**.

Or, if you take morning-star, go to **54**.

But, if you decide to take the bag of smokebombs, go to **50**.

42

Well, here you are on sunny Skraldespand . . . What do you mean that it's miserable and raining and snowing at the same time? We have no wimps in the Special Corps! Do your job and you too will soon save the universe in the manner made famous by, and I blush to say it, me.

Some facts I forgot to mention before we got here: Skraldespand is a prison planet where the dregs of a thousand worlds are dumped. No, don't press the button on your pocket matter-transmitter anymore, it won't work until you have Prof. Geisteskrank by the hand. And, no, you can't have a gun. People can get killed that way, yourself included. You have the equipment I usually carry – smokebombs, sleep gas bombs, pocket-knife, dehydrated alcohol drink, nose filters so you don't sleep-gas yourself bye-byes, five silver and five gold coins, a minimedic and two horror comics for reading when things get dull.

So goodbye and good luck. I'll be seeing you again. I hope. Turn to **62**.

Well, we all make mistakes. The mud turns out to be quicksand so you can't get out this way. You have no choice but to brave the splashing stingrays and swim to **63**.

That's it, call to Sluj, insult him – not hard to do with anyone who looks like that! He roars with rage and runs at you waving the bloodstained club. Your nerve is cool as you slip the little devices into your nostrils. He roars closer, you can feel his hot breath upon you – smell it too, ugh! Now – at the very last moment – you snap a gas grenade under his nose and step away from his falling body.

Hear the slaves cheer with joy at the brute's downfall: they cheer you as their saviour. You have the decency to blush. Arbuthnot speaks.

'Saved again – how can I ever thank you? I will do anything for you! All here are your willing servants. But ask us and we do obey!'

That sounds like an offer that you cannot refuse. Make up your mind – then turn to **22**.

Come off it! Since when do prospective members of the Corps amuse themselves by killing unarmed men? You weep a silent tear at the mistake you almost made, pat the guard on the shoulder and nobly go to **215**.

46

Now wasn't he nice? He told you to go to **193** to find Groannsville. But he could be lying. You can always go back to the crossroads at **97**.

47

You start down the steps, careful not to slip in the noxious slime. But soon the slime ends – and so do the steps. There is only a dark tunnel ahead. Well, you know what to do. Crawl. Long before terminal exhaustion sets in you see a light ahead, you crawl faster and emerge into a solid steel chamber with riveted walls. And no exit that you can find. It might be wisest to go back into the tunnel – but, no! – with a hideous crunching sound the tunnel collapses. You just got out in time. But now what? Is there something in that dark corner of the chamber? You go forward to see. Yes – there is a bright red handle protruding from the wall with a tasteful skull capping its end. Doesn't look too promising. There is something carved into the metal above the handle. Instructions in thirty-four languages, half of them long vanished. It can be translated to mean – sorry, I didn't know you could read any of them. I agree. The simplest translation would be PULL ME. Do you have a choice?

After brooding a bit you reach out quivering fingers and pull –

The floor opens. You are falling, falling down to **198**.

48

Dark, dark forest, deep forest – hey, that sounds kind of familiar . . .

> The woods are lovely, dark and deep.
> But I have promises to keep,
> And miles to go before I sleep.

That's from a poem, yes it is, written back on Dirt or Earth or whatever it was called. Do you know who wrote it? If you think it was Robert W. Service turn to **61**.

If you are sure it was written by Robert Frost turn to **67**.

49

Why should they lie at this stage? Down the stairs you go, happily jumping two at a time and there, ahead, seems safe, another room ahead . . . Peek in.

Well, looks harmless enough. A nice little well-lit chamber, a comfortable chair on wheels, the wheels on tracks leading through a tunnel to glorious sunshine. And another sign that reads, in translation of course:

UNHAPPILY THE STAR BEAST IS DEAD – BUT THANKS FOR COMING. PLEASE SIT IN THIS COMFY CAR, PRESS THE BUTTON AND YOU WILL LEAVE. HAVE A SAFE JOURNEY.

I agree – you can't trust a Kakalok. Or can you? You could sit in the chair and press the button and go to **304**. Or creep by it and walk down the tracks and get out to **337** that way. Decide!

Whistling happily and swinging your bag of smokebombs as you go, you go. Down the broken-bone road, kicking a skull along in front of you just for fun. This world has done you no good, no good at all! You are becoming as hardened as the most hardened criminal around.

Sadie was right – after less than a day's walk, you see the decayed roofs of a town over the next hill and beside the road a sign which reads:

ENDSVILLE – POPULATION 467 AND DECREASING RAPIDLY

As you read the sign you hear a scream of pain ending with a mortal gurgle and the sign clicks and the number now reads 466. This is a really tough place. But you must go on!

You start towards town – then stop as you hear heavy breathing and cursing coming towards you around the bend. Where there is heavy breathing and cursing there is usually someone doing the HB and C you reason. You will face up to the danger – no turning back now!

You take out one of the smokebombs and loop your finger through the pin, ready to throw it, your sword clutched in your other hand as you wait expectantly for **164** to appear.

You are the winner! On bended knees he pleads for mercy.

'Oh mighty stranger – you have vanquished me. It would take but a little stab of your mighty sword to polish me off and send my lifeless body plummeting into the gorge behind me. But mercy, I beg! I am a paid-up member of the Guards Union and I retire next year on half pay. Let me but live and I will tell you how to avoid the pitfalls on the far side of this chasm. Will you do that?'

Being a real sweety-pie at heart you nod and beam and go to 215.

Or are you going to be strong and guard your back? Thinking of gloom and death you step forward to 45.

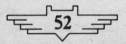

52

You sing – and oh, how you sing, putting your heart and soul into it for your life may be at stake. And when you are done and you stop for breath the mighty procuswine shakes its quills at you, rakes the ground with a giant trotter – and bursts out laughing.

'Ho-ho, weak human – you have been the butt of a swinish prank! I was going to help you in any case, but I just wanted to have one last song with you afore ye gang away. Your adventure on this disgusting planet is almost at an end. You will find out how if you turn triumphantly to 307.'

53

No, don't turn and run away! The sign says Hestelort – but it doesn't look that great. Still, you're not going to set up housekeeping here. All you need is some info on the whereabouts of the evil Prof. Geisteskrank. But take some precautions for a change, won't you? I can't feel all the knocks on the head that you have had – but looking out through your eyes gives me the impression that they are plenty bloodshot.

See the nice tavern up ahead there? What does the signboard read? THE HANGING COPPER, my, my, along with

a nice painting of a blue-coated minion of justice swinging from a gibbet. No, it is not a bad omen, don't get chicken now. You really can't expect the denizens of a prison planet to love the law. Push on! If you go in for a cooling beer turn to **139**. Or if you are getting tired of taking chances maybe you ought to see if anyone comes out and turn to **16**.

Whistling happily and spinning your morning star around your head as you go, you go. Down the broken-bone road, kicking a skull along in front of you just for fun. This world has done you no good, no good at all! You are becoming as hardened as the most hardened criminal around.

Sadie was right – after less than a day's walk you see the decayed roofs of a town over the next hill and beside the road a sign that reads:

ENDSVILLE – POPULATION 467 AND DECREASING RAPIDLY

As you read the sign you hear a scream of pain ending with a mortal gurgle and the sign clicks and the number now reads 466. This is a really tough place. But you must go on!

You start towards town – then stop as you hear heavy breathing and cursing coming towards you around the bend. Where there is heavy breathing and cursing there is usually someone doing the HB and C you reason. You will face up to the danger – no turning back now!

You clutch the handle of your morning star, give the chain a rattle, shake the spike-studded globe on the end and wait for **71** to appear.

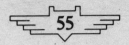

55

What a climb. But you can do it! Up and over the ridge, then down and down again to the jungle. Here the trail leads off through the squishy plants to **206**.

56

No one is listening now – so I can be brutally frank. You will never get into the Special Corps with a memory like yours. As full of holes as a colander! Take a brace and think. Remember, you were in danger, facing certain death or worse, you had three gold coins left – what did you do with them?

Great! A little prodding and it all came back. You hid them in your left boot. What a brain. Turn victoriously to **11**.

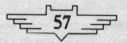

57

The sound of running footsteps ahead! You have chosen the right way to go. Run faster – you have him – for there he stands in the open doorway with nothing but air behind him. He must surrender now!

That's funny, he's gone. You look out and see that he has grabbed a rope from a beam overhead and has swung over to the castle rooftop. The rope swings back. Should you try to grab it? Looks dangerous. But that old creep made it. That's it, what courage. You seize the rope and swing out over the dizzying depths right to **255**.

The crowd roars hoarsely above, screaming obscenities and throwing beer bottles. But you ignore them – you have eyes only for your opponent. He is burly, ugly, well-muscled, scar-covered, unwashed – and wearing a shield on his left arm. More important, he has an ugly sharp sword in his right hand which he lifts above his head as he roars a battle cry.

He attacks, rushing at you, sword swinging. Don't just stand there shivering – do something! That's it, fight, fight as only fighters of the Special Corps can fight.

If you cast your net at his sword arm turn at once to **283**.

Or, if you prefer to trip him and win that way, hurl the net at his feet and rush instantly to **160**.

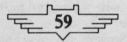

'**You're a prince**,' Robbing Good says, taking your arm in the friendliest manner possible and leading you away from the others. '**They are a lying crew – and you know that you can trust me. Well – *normally* – you can trust me, that is. But not in the matter of gold coins for which I have an endless lust.**'

Just as the impact of this statement is sinking in, the impact of his fist on the back of your head knocks you to the ground. You roll over and look at his arrow vibrating with the tension of the drawn bow, his fingers slipping from the nocked arrow . . .

Right, you don't need any diagrams to understand this. With a sigh you tell him where the coins are buried and he rushes off. Oh, gloom – you are doomed to spend the rest of your life on this planet. Well, not quite. That's it – look up. Listen to me and stop feeling sorry for yourself for one moment. There is one thing I haven't told you about yet. I was saving it for the right moment and this looks like the moment. While you were under hypnosis – you didn't know we had you hypnotized did you? The Special Corps does not reveal all its secrets! Anyway, while you were hypnotized, we planted a miniature time machine in the joint of your right index finger. All you have to do is crack your knuckle to energize it. That's it, don't feel foolish, pull hard on your finger. As soon as it goes crack you will go to **80**.

Well done! You have dodged his net, hit him with your shield and have sent him crashing to the ground. Instantly you are upon him. You stand on his back while he writhes beneath you and raise your sword high to plunge into his back. Should you? You look to the Royal Box for a sign from Sadie the Sadistic. She raises her arm slowly, and slowly you turn to **91**.

You can't be punished because poetry wasn't your big subject in school. It was by Frost. Turn to **67** and all is forgiven.

Well, oh new and frightened recruit field agent, I said that I would be seeing you again – but you won't be seeing me. Complicated? You betcha, because that's what life is like, complicated I mean. The explanation is this. I am now back in the Special Corps Main Base, with a cool drink in my hand and my head stuffed into a metal helmet. This helmet is part of a machine called an Interspacial Cortical Interpreter. Or ICI for short. No, it is not pronounced Icky! Are you a wise guy or something? You had better listen closely because, lo!, your very existence may depend upon ICI. Here's how it works.

I can look out through your eyes, see what you see – and give you sage advice. But the decisions are up to you. We shall begin and you will grow to understand the ramifications and complications of this technique.

Right now you are walking along the road going towards the woods. The rain has stopped but it is still windy – watch out for falling branches. The path winds away among the trees, the wind is keening through the boughs, pretty spooky, hmm? But it doesn't bother you, no! You're a recruit for the Corps and you laugh at danger!

Speaking of danger – you can stop laughing now! – there is movement ahead, someone is coming. That's it, stop and wait, good, a figure appears . . .

And what a figure! A lovely young lady. Now is your chance to show what you are made of! You can bug out of here – or you can smile and speak to her. Choose!

If you leave go to **14**.

If you stay for a chat go to **99**.

63

Safely ashore, you kick the last of the stingrays back into the lake and look for the balloon. There it is, sinking lower – it is down! Run, don't walk, it will help dry you off, go to **130**.

Well, the ruse seems to have worked that time. The guard is screaming and thrashing around in the smoke – he sounds angry. But he left the cell door open. You're getting the idea; crawl out on your hands and knees, feel your way down the hall. The smoke's thinning out – now run!

It's a long hall isn't it – so why are you stopping? Ohh, you hear voices – and there they are. Six soldiers – all heavily armed. You had better throw a gas bomb and go to **114**; or should you decide on a smoke bomb it will take you to **175**.

It was a tough battle, for Betsy Booster knows how to fight. But your biting her ankle gave this ugly mug the edge and she has now fled into the woods. The Brute turns to you, scowling and growling, lifting his club – and you have second thoughts. Too late! He speaks . . .

'**Oh, thank you, young gentleperson! I came to your aid to free you and you must have divined my motives.**'

He throws the club aside and snaps your chains like threads.

'**I am Arbuthnot the Rejected, led to a life of crime because the world has rejected me, sent to this prison planet for crimes too unspeakable to speak about. Only you have ever befriended me and I shall not forget that. Go in peace, dear friend – and feel that you can always count on Arbuthnot for aid!**'

After these kind words you will enjoy waving goodbye to the dear fellow and going to **48**.

Very nice, quite comfortable in fact, though this moving walkway seems to go on forever. Yes, sitting down is a good idea. But why are you starting to sweat like that? Stand again, look ahead. I'm afraid that I see it too. This moving trap goes downward and ends in a pool of molten lava.

That's it – start walking back. You can make it, this thing doesn't move very fast . . .

Thank you for correcting me. It didn't *used to* move very fast. It speeds along now, the air is getting hotter, the lava closer . . .

Then you spot it. A tiny stone platform in the lava. Your only chance. Run forward, faster and faster – then leap to **181**!

67

Well it is still pretty dark in the woods but at least you don't have to worry anymore about poetry. Walk carefully now, who knows what evil lurks among those trees . . .

What's this? The road divides into *four* ahead. That is surely an oddball way to lay out roads. Ahh, well, decisions, decisions. I hope that you haven't forgotten your mission. You should get to Groannsville to get information about Prof. Geisteskrank. But which road should you take? Don't ask me – I'm as new to this broken-down planet as you are. But hark – footsteps approach. That's it, hide behind a bush, you're learning fast.

It's an old man leaning on a staff. Maybe you should have a staff like that yourself? Come in handy, with all the bashing about around here. That's it, dig in your pocket. Get out your pocket knife.

If you use the knife to cut a staff go to **97**.

If you hold the knife as a weapon go to **146**.

68

You sing – and oh, how you sing, putting your heart and soul into it for your life may be at stake. And when you are done and you stop for breath the mighty porcuswine shakes its quills at you, rakes the ground with a giant trotter – and bursts out laughing.

'Ho-ho, weak human – you have been the butt of a swinish prank! I was going to help you in any case, but I just wanted to have one last song with you afore ye gang away. Your adventure on this disgusting planet is almost at an end. You will find out how if you turn triumphantly to 307.'

69

Help me, you cry out – and Help! again. But look at them, the clanking cowards. They flee in a panic. So much for their worthless tin hides.

You turn to flee as well – but it is too late.

A great, hairy, unwashed hand seizes you up. You are helpless in the powerful grasp. You writhe, but cannot escape as the brute paws through your clothing and finds the Jewel of the Jungle. Roaring with happiness, it ties you up with vines stripped from the trees.

This is not too good. If you want to find out what happens next you'll have to turn to **70**. Go ahead, waiting won't do any good.

Nothing much happens for the moment. The hairy brute is much taken with the Jewel of the Jungle and polishes it and stares at it and chortles a good deal. You writhe against the vines but they have been tied too tightly. Is this the end?

'This is the end!' the brute says, standing over you and laughing. 'I'm not this hairy by accident you know. I'm the first cousin of Hairy Harry the Killer Cannibal and I share all of his disgusting habits – including a taste for long pig. We only disagree on the manner of preparation. He likes a New England boiled dinner, but I think he has seen too many crappy cartoons of cannibals cooking up explorers in big black pots. Meat should be roasted, I say!'

Nor has he been idle while he has been speaking, gathering up dried branches and piling them around you right up to your neck. You gaze out over the pile of kindling as he takes out his Zippo and lights it, laughing hysterically all the time of course.

Is this it? Have you had it? Doomed to be cooked and eaten on this distant planet light years from Earth? Is this your fate?

Don't ask me when you can find out yourself. That's it, use your teeth because your hands are tied, to turn damply to 278.

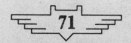

Loud footsteps sound now and around the bend comes a really ugly cowboy riding a six-legged horse.

'**Stand and deliver, you-all!**' he shouts out as he coils his rope in one hand.

He is unarmed and you hurl insults at him – which he catches and hurls back. Meanwhile he swings his lassoo around his head. Suddenly, you are not too happy. You rush to attack, but the six-legged horse is fast on his feet and skitters away. You cannot reach him with your morning star or sword and you wish you had taken the bow and arrows instead.

But it is too late to grieve! His arm lashes out and the rope snakes towards you. You dodge – but it is too late. The loop settles over your arms, trapping you and he dives and bulldogs you to the ground and disarms you. Is this the end? You can find out only by turning to **161**.

She's not being too sadistic this time for she raises her thumb – thumbs up and the rough crowd cheers wildly. Even they appreciate her good sportsmanship. You bow in her direction, give the prostrate body a last kick to show who won, then turn majestically to **335**.

This looks like a nice trail, winding away through the jungle, up hill and down. Jungle sounds on all sides – but that sort of thing doesn't frighten you! No sirree. You swing your sword swishily and whistle through your teeth.

Why are you stopping? Oh, I see, yes, it is fairly obvious now that you point it out. A great earthquake has riven this path with a mighty crack in the ground. Too wide to jump over, too deep to climb.

Not much choice is there? You don't want to go back –

what a waste of time. Yes, I see it now. A faint trail that meanders up the side of the hill. I guess you will have to meander along with it to **313**.

74

Well done. The robot rushes past you and you give the thing a swipe on the back of the head as it goes by. It falls – but springs to its feet again and advances. This time it is you who attack, screaming horribly, aiming a great blow that the robot cannot dodge. Your sword descends – and you find out what happens at **320**.

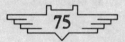

75

This bozo is a lot faster than you imagined. He is right behind you, roaring and swearing and getting closer with each bound. There is nothing for it – you are going to have to wheel about and fight.

It is sword against club and a vicious battle indeed. The brute is very strong and parries your thrusts with maniac laughter. Then he springs in and a whistling blow strikes the sword from your hand. Is all lost? You are going to have to run for it again. Better luck this time. But it is no good. He is on you in a trice. A great, hairy, unwashed hand seizes you up. You are helpless in the powerful grasp. You writhe but cannot escape as the brute paws through your clothing and finds the Jewel of the Jungle. Roaring with happiness, it ties you up with vines stripped from the trees.

This is not too good. If you want to find out what happens next you'll have to turn to **70**. Go ahead, waiting won't do any good.

76

Well done! You have cut his club in half with your sharp blade. He retreats, cursing, and draws a dagger. Then attacks again. You step back out of reach and aim a blow either at his legs – go to **310** – or if you swing at his head go to **237**.

77

Come off it! Since when do prospective members of the Corps get off destroying helpless rusty robots? You weep a silent tear at the mistake you almost made, pat the robot on the shoulder and nobly go to **78**.

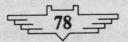

78

'Thank you, oh mighty and lenient stranger! As a reward for your justice I will tell you what you need to know. When you cross the bridge you will come to a fork in the trail. If you go left you will die within seconds, killed by the poisonous snakes that abound there. Take the right fork to safety. Now go – with a poor robot's thanks.'

Nodding acceptance of what is your due you stride across the bridge to **128**.

79

He roars with victory, thinking that he has you now, leaps forward. But you are a fighting devil you are! As he jumps you lash out with your legs and send him sprawling and falling – right back to the edge of the chasm at **51**!

Pretty fancy, hey? You have zipped back in time and are once more beneath the gallows with the volunteers for your gold coins. What they don't know is that you now know they are all a bunch of crooks. Ohh, you knew that all the time? But you have been forced into trusting them in the attempt to find the professor. So keep trying – even though you can't trust them. But don't make the same mistake twice. You have zipped back in time because of being too trusting. Don't give any of these crooks a second chance. So choose. I'll remind you what to do.

330 will take you for a ride with the Duke of Groann.

Or travel with Arbuthnot the Rejected: go to **149**.

Unless you wish to trot along to **59** with Robbing Good.

And at **21** – disgusting thought! – you will find Hairy Harry.

And the luscious Sadie the Sadistic awaits at **159**.

And I have one other bit of advice. No, I'm sorry I cannot give it to you right now. Your friends await with kind offers of help. You must give them a chance to tell you what they know. Yes, that's right, all five of them. Now don't cheat – no cheats allowed in the Corps! Try them out.

Only after you have given every one of the five a chance to help you can you turn to **168**.

Nothing good. Your blow misses and you are caught with a counter-blow. You fall. Roaring with rage your opponent attacks – but you lash out with your legs. Lash all the way to **51**.

82

You regain consciousness, alone on the rooftop. The professor of evil has gone. You have no choice, the pursuit must go on. You drag one weary foot after another through the turret door and thence to **148**.

83

Yes, twist and writhe with guilt! You call yourself a recruit for the Special Corps? Hear the old man scream! That's it – be brave – rush back to **139**.

84

You got another bullseye, while the scowling ruffian broke his arrow against a rock. He's not as good as he says he is. You have two now, hurrah! Quick – shoot another arrow. Heads is **288**, tails **166**.

85

If you said a crow with a machine-gun score thirteen points. If you got it wrong, you score nought. Now listen, he-who-breathes-forth-flame speaks again. **'Next shot. What happens when you cross an elephant with a jar of peanut butter?'** Think hard – then turn to **31**.

You're on top of the wall – no one in sight, a quick drop to the ground. Now whistling casually you stroll out into the busy castle yard . . .

What next? A lot of nasty looking people here. Just a few that don't look like criminals. The small boy – and the old lady. You want to talk to one of them? Why not. If you whisper to the kid go to **137**. Or if you are partial to old ladies go to **25**.

That was neat, the way you kicked each one in the head with the boot they were pulling. Look at all those gaping jaws! Right, creep aside quick while they grope around the spot where you used to be. Quietly, tiptoe out the door and down the hall. Faster now – for in a few seconds the charge will be gone and you will be visible again. There you go, cursing again . . . yes, I see them now. Guards filling the hall ahead, the stewpot behind. Have you looked down? You have, you've seen the handle too. Lift it quickly – they see you now.

Only darkness beneath the trapdoor. But not much choice, is there? That's it, jump down to **306**.

What a shot! Right through the pippick. It falls at your feet and expires. And about time too. These close shaves are coming a little too often for comfort. It's time that you were moving on. There is a sort of path here that seems to go in the right direction according to your sodden map and you take it. One step after another, onward ever onward . . .

Why are you stopping? I hear them now – footsteps coming down the trail in your direction.

Time for a quick decision. If you hide and peek out sneak go to **249**. But if you are tired of hiding and want to face up to this right now, why, then stand firm at **131**.

The Star Beast is getting bored with this and the prof has fallen asleep in his cage and you wish that you were someplace else – but you stir to life when the beast speaks. **'Kind of weak on the old physics, aren't you? How is your chemistry? Listen carefully to this poem:**

> Little Lucy in the lab,
> Lies dead upon the floor.
> For what she thought was H_2O,
> Was H_2SO_4.

'Got that? Now for the question: what is H_2SO_4?'
Thinking furiously you turn to **1**.

The bribe seems to have worked. The instructions were clear enough. A right turn here, then a left turn . . .

And you've walked right into the arms of the guards, who are really sort of angry. They grab you and hustle you off to **175**.

91

She's not being too sadistic this time for she raises her thumb – thumbs up and the rough crowd cheers wildly. Even they appreciate her good sportsmanship. You bow in her direction, give the prostrate body a last kick to show who won, then turn majestically to **335**.

92

There it is, right up ahead, the fine old county seat of Hestelort. No it's not, the tattered sign says Svinelort – which means the road signs have been turned around. So what do you do? Go ahead to this filthy place? If so go to **200**. Or go back and try the other road at **53**?

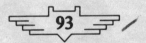

93

You slide down a chute – shoot through the air – and land on a soft mattress that emits a large cloud of dust. When you finish sneezing and dash the tear from your eyes you see that you are in an immense chamber and there, right before your eyes, is Prof. Geisteskrank. He is locked in a cage and looking fiercely unhappy. To you he never looked better. You open your mouth to speak – but before you do there is an immense roar behind you and a blast of hot air. You whirl about and see a hideous, giant, scaly, winged dragon just a few feet away!

You reel back as another blast of flaming dragon halitosis blasts out. The dragon fixes its noxious little red eyes on you, opens its smoke-stained jaws – and speaks!

'Well, look what we have here – another little squishy

mammal, just like the one in the cage! You look good enough to eat, deary – but I must control my appetite. Look, be a nice creature and shovel a few bucketfuls of coal into my mush before my fire goes out.'

You have little choice. You take the shovel from the coalbin beside you, the creature opens its horrible gaping mouth – and you shovel like crazy. You are adrip with sweat before it belches a cloud of smoke and coal gas and signals *enough* with a wave of its claws.

'That will do nice,' it burps. 'If you are hungry, too, just help yourself to a little nosh from the table over there.'

Since you never argue with a dragon, you turn to the table to see two slices of cake, one chocolate and the other coconut. As you look at them the prof calls out.

'Fashtoonking dumfkopf – the beast means to kill you. The chocolate is poisoned and the coconut contains a brain-destroying drug.'

If you listen to him and don't eat, turn to **103**. Or if you ignore the fiend, and fear not the poison and eat the chocolate go to **221**. Or if you feel that your mind has already been destroyed by this world in any case and nosh the coconut turn to **158**.

It was quite a battle – but your help turned the tide! How the thug screamed and ran away when you bit his ankle. Tasted horrible, didn't it? But enough, Betsy approaches, smiling, reaching for your chains. She speaks:

'Thanks for nothing – sucker! You still stay my slave! Ha-Ha!'

Laughing, she pulls you to your feet by the chains and boots you down the road. Are you beginning to regret your decision? Beauty is in the eye of the beholder. Maybe the ugly thug might have helped you – Betsy certainly didn't.

But – hark! – is that a noise in the woods? Is someone there? Yes, it is the ugly thug. He has not gone away. You get a second chance. Do you want to take a chance?

If you call to the thug turn to **65**.

If you do nothing turn to **7**.

You are on a small balcony looking out at the sky and the wheeling birds. Very lonely. But how about looking down and seeing what is happening. Crawling Comets – there is the evil professor escaping across the castle roof. You have no choice – even if you have no head for heights. You must climb down this wall, there're plenty of handgrips, and follow the mad prof. There you go, over the edge, you won't be able to hold on so well if your hands keep sweating like that. Better turn to **255**. Quickly.

With dragging steps you enter the alien artefact. All is strange. The floor is hard to the touch – yet is springy as turf. An alien mystery. The walls, which are soft to the touch yet not springy at all, glow with a nacreous light – why are you stopping? You want to know what nacreous means. The dictionary will tell you, we must press on. The nacreous illumination casts nacreous shadows on all sides making it difficult for you to see where you are going. But there is something ahead. Mysterious and alien, indeed – what a strange race they must have been.

There are what appears to be four ways to proceed and none of them looks attractive. Is that writing, where, there – ahh yes. Human writing with a cheap felt tip. And I recognize the style – it is the prof's. He was making notes, perhaps to help him find his way.

At the edge of this hole in the floor, with the fireman's pole in the middle, he has written **105**. The slime-covered, cold and repulsive stairway with the cold wind blowing down it is labelled **47**. While the dark tunnel, so low one would have to crawl, has a shaky **123** next to it. And look, just like an airport, a moving walkway with a triumphant **66** on it.

What to do? Which did he take? He could have lied with the labels. Over to you for decision.

97

The old man is wary – but doesn't seem to be frightened of your staff. Just don't go too close. Now question him about the roads. Louder – he's cupping his ear.

'What's that you say, young'un, the road to Groannsville? I wouldn't go there if I was you, terrible place. The old Count's hobby is torture machines. You must go, you say, well then – you'll be sorry – you take the south road.

'Louder – can't hear you. Them other roads? Why the north road goes to the dismal swamp, horrible place. East road leads to the prison warden. West road – if you're hungry – goes to the robot-operated free soup kitchen. That's all right, don't thank me – stop kissing my hand you young rascal!'

Nice old man wasn't he? Or was he? Can you trust *anyone* on this prison planet? Well, make your mind up you young rascal. Where do you go next?

If north turn to **193**.
If east go to **174**.
If south turn to **186**.
If west go to **129**.

You are in an immense slide lubricated with rushing water. Gasping and gurgling you are carried along. But the water is not running so fast now – you sit up and try to peer ahead. You hear a rushing sound and a great hissing. What can it be?

Unhappily you find out soon enough. The water trough emerges into a large chamber filled with an immense pool of lava! The trough goes down into the lava where the water is turned instantly to steam. Is this the end? You peer through the clouds of steam and see one hope, a tiny islet of rock in the lava pool. Ready . . . JUMP to **181**.

Well, we all make mistakes – and this one was a beaut. Do you wonder why it is so dark? That is because you have been knocked out with a whiff of narcogas. Now open your eyes – but you won't like what you see.

That's right. You have handcuffs on your wrists and your ankles are chained together. Admittedly, they are gold chains – but does that help? But wait, the lovely creature who trapped you is speaking . . .

'You're new here, aren't you bowb? It's easy enough to tell. Only a newcomer would let anyone get that close. My monniker is Betsy Booster, but you can call me Betsy like everyone else does. I'm called Booster because I specialized in boosting payrolls. Stealing is what they called it when they finally caught me. Sent me to this prison planet to save society from my sinister influence. Biggest mistake they ever made. I *like* it here. Life is interesting. I trap new arrivals like you and let them work for me, slave for me, and when they are burnt out husks I sell them. Ha-ha! And you will work – or else. And don't ask what the *or else* is. I shudder at the thought.

'So here we go. This road will take us to Groannsville. The Duke of Groann is raising an army – and I'll get a good price for you. Move it!'

As you stumble along in your chains, you think how lucky you have been. Yes, lucky! Betsy didn't search you – because convicted prisoners are always sent here empty-handed and unarmed. But not you!

That's it – let your hand slip into your pocket as you walk. Your fingers touch a bomb – draw it out – now!

BOOOOOMM!

But what kind of a bomb did you throw? Here's how you find out. To determine the course of future events you will need to use an amphisbenic bipolar determinator.

What, you have never heard of an APB, which is the common term for an amphisbenic bipolar determinator? You've got one right there in your change. Take it out, that's right, a real APB.

Yes, all right, it's called a coin too, an even more common term for an APB. The operating instructions are . . . Ohh? You know how to operate an APB?

That's right, flip it into the air. Let it land, look at it. If it is:

HEADS turn to **106**

TAILS turn to **189**

100

You drape the net over your left arm, seizing one end in your fist, and grab up the trident with your right hand. Are you ready? You had better be – because the door before you is grinding open, sunshine floods in. You straighten your back and march proudly to **58**.

101

So what if he bit your ankle when you talked to him? You knocked him out with an uppercut. Go to **20** and get something to eat.

102

The door leads to a clean and well-lit room. I agree, quite a change. There is a soft chair beside a table, upon which stands an immense fruit bowl. You cough and splutter as the saliva fills your mouth. It has been ages since you ate last and the fruit looks good. But shouldn't you be careful? It might be a trap or the fruit might be poisoned or something.

I'm sorry, I can't understand what you are saying. You shouldn't talk with your mouth full of fruit like that.

You have finished most of the fruit by now and the floor is littered with rinds and husks. This planet has given you some bad habits.

Belching like that and ignoring my advice are two more of those bad habits!

A creak of an opening door! You spin about, on guard,

ready for any horror that might come in. Something approaches from the darkness and enters . . . it is . . .

Yes, not quite what you expected. It is a lovely woman in a skintight gown, firm of figure and flesh. Have you ever seen her before? Yes, but only from a distance, the rich red lips speak – and you are sure.

'Welcome, stranger, welcome. I can see by your gaping jaw and bulging eyes that you recognize me – for you saw me earlier in the Royal Box in the arena. I am Sadie the Sadistic, only ruler of the Sons of Sadism. Which isn't really the right name since half of my army is female, but Sons and Daughters of Sadism doesn't quite have the same fine ring. And we live by terror!'

You shiver a bit and let your knees quake since this is obviously expected of you, and Sadie nods approval.

'I liked your style in the arena. I never saw anyone else face down a wild beast like that. Therefore I am doing you the immense favour of enrolling you in my sadistic army. You ready to join? Remember – it is enrolment or instant death. You've decided to join? Very good.

'But it's not a lifetime enrolment. I hear a lot of things and one thing I heard is that you are after that scientific nutcase named Prof. Geisteskrank. Good for you and I'll be glad to help put him out of circulation. But only after you have done a little favour for me. A quick journey through the Juicy Jungle, to a secret temple hidden among the ruins there, to find and bring back the great Jewel of the Jungle. I know that you will do it, the animals are rough – I've lost twelve volunteers – but you are number thirteen and that is a lucky number. And you have a way with animals.'

Not much choice, is there? You wisely accept her offer and proceed down the hall after her to **109**.

103

A roar of irritation from the dragon that singes your back hair sends you leaping forward for the chocolate cake and to **221**.

104

A nice wide path, well marked with sanguine insignia, you whistle as you go – my, but your morale is high, you could become a field agent after all! And there ahead of you is an orchard overgrown with yummy-looking fruit. An interesting orchard since it is filled with two kinds of fruit. They both seem identical except for their colour. One is green – the other orange. Which one will the Roc like? Beats me. You will have to make your own mind up about this.

Yes, the orange ones do look rather tasty. If this is your choice start picking at **15**.

Or if you know something about a Roc's taste in fruit and favour the green, then stroll to **314**.

Or if you want to hedge your bets and get some of both go to the middle of the orchard at **155**.

105

So sliding down the pole seemed like a good idea. But how long has the slide taken? You could never go back. And it is getting hotter, glowing reddish and nasty down below. You look down and grab tight to the pole. Because the end of the pole ends in a pool of molten lava. Don't ask me, the decision is yours. But if you would open your eyes and stop shaking like that you would see a tiny stone platform

in the lava. Yes, one chance. As you slide down you must let go, push off, jump and try to land on that tiny spot at **181**.

106

Well, some days nothing seems to go right. That was the smokebomb you grabbed. Because of your chains, you couldn't escape in the darkness – and Betsy gave you a black eye for your trouble. You're still on your way to Groannsville. But – look – there is someone else approaching!

What an ugly bloke! Fists like hams, eyes like yams, hair like a lamb's! He may sound edible but he is still nasty. He's running this way now, waving a club. Betsy is squaring off in a karate fighting mode.

There is going to be a battle. They look evenly matched. Say – if you help one of them win you may get out of this fix. So do something!

If you help Betsy turn to **94**, but if you help the thug turn to **65**.

107

Down and down this trail winds, along the hillside above a dismal swamp. Careful of your footing! One slip here and the slimy mud will hold you in its embrace forever. What sound? I didn't hear anything. Ahh, yes, I do now – a bellowing and snorting. And there is the source – in the mud wallow, right across your path. What is it? I wouldn't like to say for sure, but it looks very much like a porcuswine. Very rare.

What to do now? Your choice. You can skirt it by going uphill to **145**. Or if you think you can slip past it better by going downhill, creep at once to **111**. Or, if you want to brave it out, sneak to **110** where you can peek out at the handsome creature from behind that tree.

Well, that wasn't much good. You tried to sneak around the hideous porcuswine but it was no good. Better creep up and take a closer look at the thing. Silently then on tiptoe to **110**.

'**Give this volunteer weapons and armour!**' Sadie orders and her minions rush to obey. '**And the secret map of Juicy Jungle that shows the way to the ruins.**'

She sweeps out regally while all bow and kowtow. It really helps when the boss is on your side. You are given stainless steel chainmail, heavy, but it will protect you. A steel helmet with a red feather – very elegant – and a sword as well as a bow and arrow. A bottle of wine, two sandwiches and a package of cookies. What more could you possibly need?

Off this screwball planet and home. Yes, I agree. And that reward will be yours as soon as you bring in the prof. So wave goodbye to the lackies. Now, with your head up and walking proudly, stamp across the bridge to the jungle at **125**.

110

Wow! Now that is what I call a real ugly! A hideous cross between a debauched pig and a quill-shedding porcupine. I've never seen anything that repulsive, even after a binge of drinking Altarian Panther Sweat. It's wallowing in the mud and making some kind of bubbling noise. Sneak closer, behind that next tree at **207** and maybe you can make out what the sound is.

111

You are right, the track is getting muddier and muddier, cloying and holding your tired legs. It's no go – you'll never get through down here. But look, there ahead, a ridge of higher land that leads up out of the swamp. Clamber on to it, and crawl along it slowly and painfully, all the way to **108**.

112

The creature again. I agree, it is a little clumsy, but all it needs is one crunch of those mighty jaws and you have had it.

You are going to do *what?* Stare it down? Prove that human beings can master the creatures of the forest with steely gaze and power of will? That is really a crazy – I mean *great* idea! Good luck – for here it comes again. Raging and tearing up the sand, teeth gleaming in the fitful sunshine, closer and closer . . .

You stand your ground, fixing it with your firm gaze and, still standing and staring, proceed to **305**.

The path climbs up through the jungle and you are staggering under the weight of the fruit. But you go on! Never stopping, even when the trail becomes steps carved into the trunk of a giant tree. Higher and higher you climb until the steps emerge on to the top of a large bough. This is some tree – the branch is as wide as a highway. And at the far end of the branch is a nest. And on the nest is, well, I guess it's a bird. If birds can be as big as airliners. You step back – but too late! – you have been seen!

The creature hurls itself into the air, the flap of its wings is like thunder. It blots out the sun – then the branch creaks and bends as it lands.

You find yourself looking up with horror into an avian eyeball the size of a pool table. The great yellow beak opens and in a voice of thunder the Roc speaks.

'Well, hello – and what do we have here? A toothsome little morsel who looks like a walking fruitstand. Dare I ask, little munchy, just what you are doing with all that yummy fruit?'

That's it, don't by shy, hold up the fruit and state your price. The eyeball comes close and the beak clacks angrily. The Roc speaks again:

'Bribery – is that what it is?! You attempt to buy the services of the Roc of Ages with this tiny offering? Well, why not. Hurl them into the air and I'll grab them. Then we go flyies. About time I did a tour of the jungle to instil fear into the denizens and install a few of them into my stomach. I hear tell there is a nest of giant snakes nearby. Sounds like a neat idea for a good spaghetti lunch.'

The big bird snaps up the fruit in an instant, then grabs you with its beak and flips you up on to its neck. Once you

are in place, it plunges off the tree and you both flap off to
199.

I can understand your being a little bitter – but did you
have to walk on top of the unconscious bodies? What do
you mean shut up? Is that a way to speak to your superior
officer. What are you doing now?

Ahh, so. An open window, a careful look outside, no
one in sight, a quick drop to the ground. Now whistling
casually, you stroll out into the busy castle yard . . .

What next? A lot of nasty looking people here. Just a
few that don't look like criminals. The small boy – and the
old lady. You want to talk to one of them? Why not.

If you whisper to the kid go to **137**.

Or if you are partial to old ladies turn to **25**.

A chamber in the rock – but before you can examine it the
floor gives way and you are falling, sliding, shooting out
through the air to land heavily in the sand. The sun hurts
your eyes. You have seen this all before you realize leadenly
as you turn to **96**.

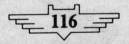

You gasp at the apparition that appears – no wonder it was
breathing heavily! A creature – could it be a man? – who
knows – stands before you dressed in homemade steel
armour. From inside the helmet an echoing voice cries out:

'Stand and deliver, stranger – or it is curtains for you!'
Followed by a very dirty laugh.

You turn and run – but this geezer is very fast on his feet and clanks around and cuts you off.

The bow! You shoot an arrow that splinters on his armour. More wild laughter. You swing with your sword which breaks in half.

I'm sorry – but you have had it. You flee once more but foul hands seize you . . . if you wish to learn what cruel fate has in store then turn, reluctantly, to **185**.

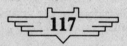

That's it – pull on the thing's neck – harder! It's turning, heading for the tower – but too low! It's going to crash . . .

Wow! This Roc of Ages must have subconscious sonar. Even when it's asleep it doesn't crash. With a single flap it lifted up and settled on the top of the tower in a perfect belly-landing.

What's that sound? Either the thing is snoring or grumbling. Don't hang around to find out. Slip down on to the top of the tower, draw your sword – not a bad idea since you don't know if this is the correct tower that leads to the Jewel – or the one that leads to certain death. About time you found out – head for the trapdoor. It creaks when it opens and a puff of dank gas comes out. No, it doesn't look too nice down there . . .

'**Stop, you poisoning pismire! You'll not escape a horrible lingering death that easily!**'

Yes, the Roc is awake and in quite a temper! Beak clashing, claws tearing grooves in the solid rock of the tower!

Say, you can really move fast when you want to! Through the trapdoor, bolt it behind you and down the steps two at a time. That kingsize sparrow is really annoyed. You can still hear him roaring and scratching, the whole tower is shaking. He'll have it down in a minute! Jump three steps at a time – why not! Rocks breaking loose, cracks in the wall – but there is the bottom and a door ahead.

Roaring and crashing? Now that you mention it, I do hear something awful coming from behind the door. But I also know that the tower is falling in. Better the devil you don't know than the devil you do. Sword ready – jump!

Right to 142.

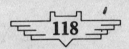

118

Once more through the bone-littered halls to the throne room. Hairy Harry belches approval at the sight of the slaves, a peregrinating pantry to him. But what a surprise he has in store! As Arbuthnot belts him with club you and all the others cast off your chains. While they beat up on the surprised guards you dart after Prof. Geisteskrank. He sees you and curses in a guttural language – which it is just as well you don't understand, because I do and it's pretty nasty stuff – and darts away.

After him! Across the throne room and through a door. Curses – he slams it in your face! Do you search for a key by going to 36, or do you grab up an ironbound club to see if you can break it down on 120.

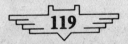

119

Some leap! You must have springs in your heels. As the door opened so did a trapdoor in the floor. Instead of falling into it you jumped over it and landed safely in the room. And there is the Jewel of the Jungle resting on the table! A ruby the size of a hen's egg, set into a nice golden

crown. No wonder Sadie the Sadistic wants it. It's the same colour as her eyes.

You step forward and reach for it – then stop.

Good thinking, because this looks too easy. Anything might happen if you just picked it up.

If you are brave and laugh at danger pick up the Jewel at **248**.

Or if you are chicken and want to live longer – reach out carefully and snare the crown with the tip of your sword on **165**.

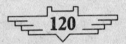

120

Thud! Crash! And the door splinters beneath your mighty blows, falling into teeny splinters at the strength of your attack. You step through the ruins, taking the ironbound club as a wise precaution, and at once face a problem.

The hall branches into three before you. What to do? Don't ask me – this is your case. Ready? You go left to **57**, or straight ahead to **39**, while the right hand leads to **276**. Go!

121

How loathsome! Hairy Harry the Killer Cannibal sits before you on a throne made of human bones – how many poor souls he must have consumed! He wears no clothes for his long, curly red hair with which he is coated conceals his vile form well enough. He speaks, in an evil voice redolent of kitchen ladles and garbage can lids.

'Ho, ho – what have we here! A toothsome morsel indeed. Off to the kitchen with him!'

But before the order can be obeyed a skinny, grey-haired

man strides in, a monocle tucked into one eye. It is Prof. Geisteskrank! He speaks . . .

'Achh, all you tink of iss your rumbling tum, Hairy Harry. I need a volunteer for a hideous experiment. Let me have this one.'

Some prospect. Out with your trusty APB and flip. Heads to **37** and the prof, tails to **18** and the stove. Life can be like that at times.

122

Like a bird you soar – up, up and away! And land with a crashing thud on the ledge which begins to break away from the rock wall behind it . . .

You really do move quite fast when you want to. Leaping, scrambling – and cursing when a drop of lava lands sizzling on your leg, you dance along the collapsing rock towards a gaping tunnel entrance and simply hurl yourself to **333**.

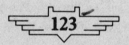

123

Take a deep breath – and crawl into the tunnel. It's pretty boring stuff, even though it is a little cramped. But the ceiling is higher now, and you can walk upright, trailing your fingers along the wall as you go, in order to find your way in the darkness.

Does it go on forever – or does it just seem that way? A little rest is surely in order, even a little nap . . .

You awake and go on. The tunnel seems endless. But just when you despair and think of turning back you see light ahead. Can it be an illusion? No, it is real, you grope the wall as you break into a run, emerging from your tunnel trap into a chamber . . .

Off of which lead two low, dark tunnels.

I know, it's one of those days. They are identical, so perhaps you had better use your APB or coin to suss this one out. Heads to **191**, tails to **17**.

124

Perhaps a wise decision – all the signs so far seem to have lied. Climb slowly, seems safe enough, another room ahead . . . Peek in.

Well, looks harmless enough. A nice little well-lit chamber, a comfortable chair on wheels, the wheels on tracks leading through a tunnel to glorious sunshine. And another sign that reads, in translation, of course:

UNHAPPILY THE STAR BEAST IS DEAD – BUT THANKS FOR COMING. PLEASE SIT IN THIS COMFY CAR, PRESS THE BUTTON AND YOU WILL LEAVE. HAVE A SAFE JOURNEY.

I agree – you can't trust a Kakalok. Or can you? You could sit in the chair and press the button and go to **304**. Or creep by it and walk down the tracks and get out to **337** that way. Decide!

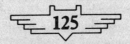

125

Dark and scary – but that doesn't bother you! Not you with your armour and your weapons and your morale bucked up by the fact that you have already knocked back half of the bottle of wine. Not that I'm complaining, mind you, just a friendly comment, ha-ha.

Animals rustle on all sides, hidden by the undergrowth, birds call out sharply from the jungle canopy above and – that's it, move aside sharply, it missed – from time to time they send little cloacal messages down to you. So why are you stopping now, not tired already?

Ahh, yes, I see, the trail has come to a junction and it now offers you three possibilities. Nor is the map any help, since all of the trails seem to go in the right direction, towards the ruins. So – the decision is up to you.

If you decide to take the trail to the left step out smartly to **107**. The central path wends its way to **206**, while the stony track on the right winds uphill to **55**.

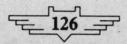

There are some days when nothing you do turns out right. Before you can get close enough to stop him, the prof cuts the rope and, screaming hysterically – or falling in grim and noble silence – you go irrevocably to **136**.

Off the trail and among the bushes, a flowery bed where you will not be seen. Darkness falls and you are content. You polish off the wine, munch the last of the sandwiches, nibble a bit on the cookies – and drift off into a restful and dreamless sleep.

Animal noises during the night disturb you. You awake, look around, see nothing and go back to sleep. It is dawn when you awake again.

With a headache from the cheap wine and a taste in your mouth like the bottom of a parrot's cage, you smack your lips and spit out little pieces of things. The ants have crawled into your cookies and you are in a foul mood, which is not improved in the slightest when you crawl forward to look at the bridge.

The guard is gone, he sure is. But in his place is a

hideous rusty robot, also armed with a great club. Maybe you should have settled on the human defender. Too late to cry over spilt milk. You gird up your loins, draw your sword – then tramp determinedly down the hill to 252.

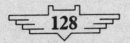

The first thing that you discover after crossing the bridge is that you have been lied to once again. There is no fork in the trail – in fact the trail becomes a ladder in the cliff that you must climb down. For a moment you consider going back and committing murder – but realize that that is far from being a constructive idea. So instead you start down the ladder, downward and downward until you enter the clouds. You hear a roaring below and, when you emerge from the clouds, you see a river below you. Very interesting.

Even more interesting is the fact that the ladder suddenly ends a good fifty metres above the water . . .

My, my, what an interesting vocabulary you have developed on this planet! What to do? I suggest you hook an arm over a rung and rest your tired limbs and look over the possibilities.

Yes, they are limited – aren't they? You could climb back to the top again – but you are so tired there is a good chance you might not make it.

Then you could let go and drop into the river and swim to safety. But if you wear your nice metal armour, you will sink to the bottom like a stone. If you take it off you will no longer have its protection.

That's it, I guess. Over to you for the big decision.

If you choose to climb, why climb then to **301**.

If you dive into the river with all of your armour on, splash into **336**.

Or if you take off your armour, keeping only your sword and bow and arrow for the dive thence to **271**.

129

What a road! Dusty, awful – but you are strong and fearless – trudge on. You have no choice, keep trudging until you get to **180**. You will enjoy being there . . .

130

You see the collapsed balloon and grow wary. After all the prof still has that gun. You must circle the balloon stealthily, either upwind to the right by going to **256**, or downwind to the left to **192**.

131

This is it! The leaves are brushed aside and you are face-to-face with a tall stranger. He is dressed in green, a little shabby and gravy-stained but, yes, it once was green. He glowers at you and shakes his longbow in your direction and speaks.

'Who is this intruder that dares intrude in the forest of **Robbing Good. That's me. I steal from the rich, and the poor – and keep all the loot for myself. And now I shall take all your loot, stranger, for you do not dare stand against me!'**

But you, you strong-hearted fool!, you do dare to stand against him. As he whips out his bow you whip out yours. As he nocks an arrow you nock yours. He draws, you draw. He aims – you aim . . .

If you really want to know how this Texas standoff ends

turn slowly to **172**. Not easy to do without taking your eyes off of him.

132

'And why should I do a scrawny punk like you a favour?' the thug growls in a voice as deep as an underground sewer. Smells like one as well. 'I should beat you up – but I'm tired after two murders in one day. You may buy your information – and your life – for the special this-week-only bargain price of one silver coin.'

Discretion being the better part of valour, and you are also tired from your recent strenuous adventures in the underground city, you smile and pay up. Suspicious as ever, this creature bites the coin, then points.

'He went thataway. I saw him grabbed by the pressgang for the arena.'

Before you can ask him just what in bowb he is talking about he screams horribly and runs off. You have no recourse but to go thataway as well to **190**.

133

Don't hang your head in shame. So you missed, so what? So you missed two in a row. So what? So he is neck and neck with you and you have to hit this next one or you lose. So don't think about it. Draw and fire and heads to **9**, tails to **286**. And good luck . . .

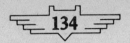

134

That nice young man with his back to the tree has a kind of crunched leg. But that is his problem – not yours. You have the galaxy to save, don't forget. Move back to the path at **169**. This has nothing to do with you.

Or if you insist on poking your nose into his affairs turn to **38**.

135

With your last strength you haul yourself from the water and sprawl almost senseless on the sandbank. These close calls are getting to be a little too much for you. Your head swims and fatigue clutches you – but you are young, strong and healthy and the effects of the cheap wine have worn off. Strength returned you climb to your feet and turn and . . .

You find yourself staring at an incredibly evil-looking creature with eyes the size of soup plates, teeth like daggers, tentacles like ropes – and terminal halitosis. You don't know what it is? Unhappily I do. Yes, I'll tell you, just don't screech like that. It is the rare and deadly Green Pippick Monster – see the green pippick on its extended and gross belly? Very poisonous. You must try to kill it with a well-placed arrow – or flee before it attacks.

That's it, slip your hand into your pocket and take out your APB. Also called a coin. My goodness, it's getting rusty, what are they making coins out of these days! That's it, flip it silently and look at it.

If it is heads go quickly to **13**.

If it's tails slip in silence to **230**.

136

The rope is cut! You fall, is this the end? No – for there is a lake below. Though while it is small and filled with stingrays it is nevertheless big enough to break your fall.

Splash – and you are down. The first stingrays zero in on you splashing their stings against the water with victorious smacks.

To the left the shore is close and muddy; to get there go to **43**. Or to reach the distant sandy beach to the right go to **63**.

137

Why does the kid look so frightened and shy away from you? Have you bathed lately? No, that is not the reason you believe, it is because this is a world of violence and everyone is afraid of everyone else. Not a very profound observation, but you are probably right. So what do you do? Play the role like everyone else and twist the kid's arm so he'll tell you where to find Prof. Geisteskrank? Or do you want to bribe him with a small coin?

A bribe will get you to **90**, while a twist of the arm and a shrill scream will land you on **167**.

138

Run! Fast as you can! This is a mistake – back where you just came from – **134**!

139

You walk casually into the bar and discover that the revelry you heard was really the sound of four thugs beating up on the tavern-keeper. They look at you and shake their clubs menacingly. You look at them and quickly make your mind up. You can stay out of trouble by leaving and going to **83** – or you can sort things out now by flipping a gas bomb at them to stop the mayhem – and then to **170**.

140

The gallows. Pretty spooky with the wind whistling through the nearby tombstones, an owl calling out Whoo-Whoo. I don't know who. The first light of dawn on the distant horizon as you scratch busily with a broken stick right behind the gallows. Very neat. The hole dug, the coins dumped, the dirt put back, the ground stamped down so that it looks as though it had never been disturbed, a few leaves and a dead beetle spread neatly over. Well done. Now all you must do is wait for dawn and see who comes.

You are tired. You sit down with your back to the gallows. My but you have guts! To sleep in a spooky place like this. What? Not guts you say, just fatigue. You nod off . . .

And when you awake you are on **179**.

141

It worked fine in the arena so it should work here. Your proud gaze has quelled the noble lion and brought the wild wolf to heel. What worked on them will undoubtedly work on this simple porcuswine. It roars close but you are not afraid! You level your finger at the beast and order it to stop.

Ouch! That must have hurt. With a twist of its cruel head it has hurled you right back to **260** to enable you to decide on a better course of action this time.

142

You dive through the door and slam it shut behind you – and just in time for there is a crunching roar as the tower falls in. The door shakes and bounces as the stones from above crash against it. You hear a terrible sound behind you – you turn and see . . .

Yipes! It is a giant tiglon sharpening its claws on the rock wall. It hears you and wheels about and roars again – look at those teeth!

You raise your sword as it attacks. What a puny defence against a creature this size. One of its teeth is longer than the sword. I have an idea . . .

Oh, you don't want to hear my idea. All right then, stand and fight at **177**, I don't care.

Though, if you would like a bit of sage advice turn at once to **171**.

143

You have very strong hands, but even you feel your grip weakening. Things don't look too good – but there, up ahead, a storm cloud. We are drifting towards it, are beneath it – and it is pouring with rain. That is good news, even if you don't believe it. With the cloud blocking the sun and the rain cooling the balloon the gas inside is cooling down. So the balloon is dropping. Your voyage may be at an end.

Sooner than you think. Prof. Geisteskrank leans over the side to look at the ground – and he has seen you!

'**Donnervetter, geshtinkerplotz!**' he curses terribly. And, see, he has a knife to cut the rope you are hanging from. If you wait, helplessly, for your certain end turn to **136**.

If you climb the rope to grapple with the nutter turn to **126**.

144

The crowd roars hoarsely above, screaming obscenities and throwing beer bottles. But you ignore them – have eyes only for your opponent. He is burly, ugly, well-muscled, scar-covered, unwashed – and carrying a net over his left arm. More important, he has an ugly trident in his right hand which he lifts above his head as he roars a battle cry.

He attacks, rushing at you, net swinging. Don't just stand there shivering – do something! That's it, fight, fight as only fighter of the Special Corps can fight.

If you try to cut his net turn at once to **282**.

Or, if you prefer to dodge out of the way and have a try with your shield and sword rush instantly to **60**.

145

Very rough going, I'll agree with that. The path has vanished and it is hard climbing this hill in the sun with all those weapons and armour.

Why are you shouting? I see, the rocks are slipping out from under you. Try as hard as you can you cannot stop your fall.

So tumble and slide all the way to **108**.

Some people just never learn. Violence doth breed violence, yeah, verily. The little old man was so frightened by your knife that he bashed you over your head and fled. Remember, this planet is covered with convicted criminals, so anyone with a weapon will be considered an attacker.

That's it – look sheepish and put the knife away. No, hold it! Cut a staff first. That will give you protection without your appearing to be threatening.

Finished? Good. Since you have frightened off the only help you have had, why you'll just have to guess which road to take:

If north to **193**.
If east to **174**.
If south to **186**.
If west to **129**.

Sadie surely has a heart of gold. Or rather a pocketful. The sadistic business must have been good lately. She shakes ten gold coins into your greedy palm and points at the horizon.

'A good day's march in that direction – following the path marked with skulls and broken bones – will bring you to the town of Endsville. Without a doubt this is the most disgusting and depraved county seat on the entire planet, where only the totally rejected, unwanted, loathsome and repugnant types go. They make the rest of us look like angels, let me tell you. Rumour has it that your potty prof Geisteskrank is holed up there and indulging in experiments too foul to mention. Do us all a favour and get him out of here. He gives ordinary criminals a bad name.'

At this point one of Sadie's minions rushes up with a basket of roast chickens and you all tuck in for a greasy feed. And while you eat you think – I hope. You feel very vulnerable with all the gold you have and all the crooks around and, when no one is looking, you slip three of the coins into your left boot.

When the ground is littered with bones and bits of skin, you belch delicately behind your hand and prepare to leave.

If you thank Sadie for her many kindnesses, stroll leisurely off to **319**.

If you want to presume on her hospitality some more for help in your mission go to **41**.

148

What is that? Oh, horrors – he has a balloon in the courtyard and he is in the basket and cutting the rope that holds it down. Now, when he is distracted – run! The balloon is rising, you jump, grab, yes – you have it.

You cling fiercely to the rope as the balloon sails high into the sky. All the prof has to do is look over and he will see you. But he does not. He is humming an obscene song and crunching something. Chicken bones drop by you. The fiend is having lunch while your hands grow stiff and cold. You breathe softly lest he hear you. Where will this end? You know – I'm interested too. At once, while you still have the strength in your fingers, turn to **143**.

With a tear in one ugly eye, Arbuthnot puts his arm around you and leads you away from the watching ruffians. He speaks:

'Dear friend, I shall be ever grateful to you. The one person in this awful world who did not reject me. How nice you are! That's it, down this path into the woods – I don't want those beastly criminals to hear what I have to say. Because what I have to say is *so* embarrassing it shames me to speak. See! I blush at the thought. But I have no choice. I must do a naughty to the only person who ever helped me!'

As you ponder the meaning of this strange statement, he hurls you to the ground with one mighty hand and raises his club over his head and snarls at you.

'One chance – and one alone, sucker! Tell me where the gold coins are – you have exactly two seconds – or I bash your brains all over the greensward. Speak!'

Rightly enough – you speak. You have no choice. Crying with happiness, he rushes away. Depressed, you hang your head.

Hist! Listen to me and stop feeling sorry for yourself for one moment. There is one thing I haven't told you about yet. I was saving it for the right moment and this looks like the moment. While you were under hypnosis – you didn't know we had you hypnotized did you? The Special Corps does not reveal all its secrets! Anyway, while you were hypnotized, we planted a miniature time machine in the joint of your right index finger. All you have to do is crack your knuckle to energize it. That's it, don't feel foolish, pull hard on your finger. As soon as it goes crack you will go to **80**.

150

The sign was an outright lie because no instant death grabs
you – nor a lingering death either. More steps, more musty
smells and scratching of fleeing and unseen rats. Another
door ahead, just enough light from the cracks in the walls
to read what is painted there:

THE JOOL ROOM – KEEP OUT!

Right, they can't spell very well – but maybe they are
better jewellers. Throw the door open and leap through
gracefully to **119**.

151

They bid you tearful goodbyes – and you wipe the oil off
your hands as soon as their backs are turned. What a
shower! You are better off rid of them. But at least one of
them, the robot pilot, knew the way to the realm of Sadie
the Sadistic. He pointed the way, directly towards the
setting sun, and you now march off strongly in that
direction. March all afternoon until you reach **270**.

152

Yes, I agree, tickling wasn't the world's greatest idea. The
great ugly creature simply brushed you aside but at least it
didn't bite you or maul you. And here it comes again!

You jump aside so that it misses you and jump right to
112.

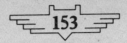

153

You could have picked a better place to climb the wall.
You landed right in front of the Enlisted Torturer's Mess
and they are a tough bunch. Bang, crash, and they have
you and you have no recourse but to turn to **28**.

154

The two of you scowl at each other, shake your weapons
and call out filthy oaths. My goodness, where did you learn
to swear like that! But no one feels like a fight and he
passes by. When you are sure that he has gone, you
continue warily down the road through the woods until
you come to a fork in the road. Out with the Old Reliable
APB and heads will take you to **176**, tails to **190**.

155

This is hard work. The big orange and green fruit are each
about the size of a grapefruit, only the wrong colour, of
course. They are high in the trees and you have to climb
up to get them. Each one is attached by a tough stem that
will not break. You try cutting one off with your sword –
and it works fine.

Except the fruit plunges to the ground and explodes
with a juicy splosh. Be more careful next time. Hold the
stem, then cut it – that's it. Then climb down carefully and
place the fruit on the ground. And climb the tree for more.

Time passes slowly until you have all that you can carry
on the ground. With a bit of vine you tie all their stems

together, hoist the orange and green bundle over your shoulder – and stumble fruitily to **113**.

156

There is a heavy clunk and Hairy Harry lets go of you – and staggers around holding his head and yiping with pain and generally feeling sorry for himself. For standing there, still swinging the club with which he has bashed Hairy Harry, is an ugly but familiar figure. It is your old chum Arbuthnot the Rejected. Listen – for he speaks!

'**To see you again, dear friend, is always a pleasure for you are the only one who has ever befriended me. Therefore I will earn the three gold coins by taking you at once to Professor Geisteskrank.**'

Before you can take up his offer, he is shouldered aside by a very sexy shoulder covered by a torn silk dress. It is Sadie the Sadistic – but she is not looking too great.

'**Listen, oh stranger, to my tale of woe. I have come down in the world, rejected by the Sons of Sadism after the arena collapsed during a minor earthquake. I walk the roads, penniless and in despair. But I have a bright future – particularly if I have three gold coins as a stake. You can trust me – for I freed you didn't I? I'll take you to the prof and claim my reward.**'

Before you can make up your mind there is a shower of leaves from a nearby tree, followed by a heavy thud as Robbing Good drops to the ground.

'**Don't listen to that sadistic tart!**' he calls out. '**She would steal the pennies from a dead man's eyes. In fact, that's just how she got the stake to found her mob. Stick with me kid – didn't I tell you the truth last time we met? And I'm the only person who knows where the professor is hiding.**'

They all shout at you and at one another – then scatter

as a great horse thunders up, hooves hammering the ground. From his back springs down an elegant figure dressed in chainmail with a gilded codpiece. He removes his helmet and you gaze at the noble features of the Duke of Groann.

'Begone, varlets,' he orders. 'You are all criminals and liars who pester this honest person. I, who am incredibly rich and don't need the gold anyway, will lead the way to the professor for I wish him removed from this planet. I need those gold coins not, for I am loaded with gelt as you can see. I will do the job.'

With this they all begin shouting at each other and arguing – which gives you a chance to make up your mind.

The Duke sure looks rich so maybe he is not lying. If you want to go with him jump on the horse behind him and gallop to **330**.

But then again you have always had good luck with Arbuthnot the Rejected. He has saved your life because you are the only person who never rejected him. Don't start now or he might cry! Go with him to **149**.

Also – Robbing Good didn't lie to you. If you want to take a chance on this forest hoodlum, spring to **59**.

But shouldn't you consider Hairy Harry, perhaps as a last resort. Anyone that evil doesn't have to lie. Let him lead you to the prof at **21**.

Though there is still Sadie the Sadistic, once kind to you, now come down in the world. Take that delicate pink hand and let her show you the way to **159**.

The decision is yours!

157

It is sword against club and a vicious battle indeed. The brute is very strong and parries your thrusts with maniac laughter. Then he springs in and a whistling blow strikes the sword from your hand. Is all lost? Should you run quickly to escape this brute? If so run to **275**.

Or why not call to the robots for help? You saved them so it should be their turn to save you. Call out to them at **69**.

You shouldn't trust that professorial nutter any further than you can throw him with one hand. You finish the cake and turn back to the dragon at **299**.

Ahh, Sadie, you lovely creature. To hold your delicate hand and trip across the greensward is paradise enow.

Why do we stop in this glade? Why does she smile and look at you so endearingly? What could she have on that lovely mind? What does she hold in those sweet fingers?

A razor-sharp knife that she has pulled from some place of concealment! You try to dash it from her hand but she is a mistress of karate. In an instant you are on the ground, the blade to your throat, her soft voice whispering in your ear:

'Talk, sucker, or you will never speak again! Where is the gold?'

You speak quickly for you have no choice. A rustle of silky garments and she is gone. You sit on the ground immersed in a sea of gloom. Well swim to the surface for a second and hear what I have to say. It appears now that there is one tiny thing I haven't told you about yet. I was saving it for the right moment and this looks like the moment. While you were under hypnosis – you didn't know we had you hypnotized did you? The Special Corps does not reveal all its secrets! Anyway, while you were hypnotized, we planted a miniature time machine in the joint of your right index finger. All you have to do is crack your knuckle to energize it. That's it, don't feel foolish, pull hard on your finger. As soon as it goes crack, you will go to **80**.

160

Well done! You have trapped his feet and sent him crashing to the ground. Instantly, you are upon him, tangling him in the net so that he cannot escape. You stand on his back while he writhes beneath you – and you raise your trident high to plunge into his back. Should you? You look to the Royal Box for a sign from Sadie the Sadistic. She raises her arm slowly, and slowly you turn to **72**.

161

Ouch! This guy is really rough. He knocks you on the head and you lie, half-stunned, as he steals everything. Morning star and sword, then he roots through your pockets. The matter-transmitter doesn't interest him, but he takes everything else that you have. Including the seven gold coins.

And when he is all done, just to add insult to injury, he unwraps his rope and before you can get up he throws you over a nearby cliff and gallops off.

But you are not dead yet! You clutch at the roots that project from the cliff, hanging on for dear life and only when the thug has gone do you pull yourself back up with the last of your energy, right to **328**.

162

NO! HORRORS! UNBELIEVABLE!!!

This is too awful to describe! Return at once to the place from whence you came.

163

So you missed. You can't win them all. Grit your teeth, take careful aim and let fly – to **84** with heads or **289** with tails.

164

What a ghastly sight! Over the hill strides a really ugly customer covered with scars, brass knuckles adorning his great fists. He looks at you and sneers loudly. You look at him and sneer back – but you are not sneering at the giant boa constrictor draped around his neck. It flicks its evil little tongue at you and sneers as well.

'Give me everything you got or my little Pansy will crush every bone in your body. Give!'

How you wish you had taken the morning star to bean this moron and his sickening serpent – or the bow to shoot them – but you did not. You will have to make do with the smokebombs. You scream and hurl one at him and he curses and retreats. So far so good. But look – he drops the snake and points:

'Go Pansy, attack and crush!'

You hurl more smokebombs until you discover something interesting about snakes. They don't see too well. But they sure can smell things and they smell with their

tongues. Straight at you out of the cloud of smoke comes
Pansy! You run – but cannot escape. In an instant she is
wrapped around you in a bone-crushing embrace and dirty
laughter tears at your ears.

How will this end? You will find out at **329**.

165

Zoom – thunk! As you lift the crown with your sword, a
hidden mechanism is released and a spear shoots down
from the ceiling and thuds into the floor – hitting the spot
where you would have been standing if you had grabbed
the thing with your hands. These ancient builders were a
murderous lot!

You slip the Jewel of the Jungle inside your jacket and
leave. This place is definitely not healthy.

Ignoring the scurrying and squeaking, you make your
way back up through the ruined place until you see a wide
crack in one wall with green leaves growing in through it.
A way out!

But you know enough about this planet now not to rush
into anything sudden-like. Before you climb out you take a
careful look. What do you see when you peer out through
the crack?

If you want to find out turn inspectorily to **311**.

166

So who said that you can win them all? You missed, and he
is creeping up on you. All you need is one more bullseye
and you are home free. Aim and shoot, that's the way.
Heads to **5**, tails to **133**.

167

You're a bit of a sadist, aren't you? Yes, I understand you weren't before you came to this pesky planet. But at least the arm twist seems to have elicited some response. Leave us hope that it is the right one. Over the castle wall, south on the road, then look for a crossroads with a sign pointing towards Hestelort. That's where the prof is supposed to hang out. There's the crossroads now – but there is also a sign pointing to Svinelort. Now the point is – should you believe your torture-extracted confession? Over to you.

If you choose Hestelort go to **92**.

If you lack faith then go to **53** and Svinelort instead.

168

A pretty rough lot – aren't they? You have given each one of them a chance to help you find the prof and each one of them has betrayed you. There they stand smirking and simpering, not knowing that you have travelled back through time, after having been betrayed by all of them.

You make your excuses. You say that you are going for the gold coins, don't go away, then walk off whistling through the forest. Then run for it!

There is crashing and loud cries behind you – but you escape. You have done it – outwitted the lot! You will hide here in the forest until dark then go back and dig up the coins and try another plan. You aren't licked yet!

You sleep for a while and when you awake the sun is low in the sky. You steal back through the woods and look out. They are gone!

Fast as lightning you dig up the gold and run for it, into the forest one last time. But – hark! – you are being followed! Something large and crashing is on your trail, coming ever closer!

It has arrived – you cannot escape! You turn about and see . . .

You don't know? You'll find out quickly enough as, with trembling fingers, you turn to **323**.

What a nice day for a stroll. Sun shining, birds cheeping their brains out. And your conscience bothers you, you say? I don't wonder – leaving that poor lad there like that. A real Field Agent would have gone to his aid. So who told you to take my bad advice? Argue later, after you have gone to **38**.

Well done. They all went nighty-night when the bomb went off, and by the time they woke up you had them bound with their own belts. You also collected six knives, two guns, a club, some chewing gum, a calendar filled with nudes, as well as a morning-star – and six copper coins. All of which you gave to the innkeeper when he came to. He is pathetically grateful when he speaks.

'**Oh, good samaritan, never did I think I would ever see a helpful deed done on this pestilential planet. For your future safety I now give you my invisibility belt which has three charges left in it. Just press the buckle and twist and you will be invisible for three minutes each time.**'

You are touched by his goodwill, buckle the belt on – but before you leave you ask him if he has heard of Prof. Geisteskrank. He nods and moans his answer:

'**The whole world knows this mad genius. He is in the employ of Hairy Harry the Killer Cannibal. Hairy Harry**

is the master of Crapper's Castle, once the demesne of that noble breed of sanitary engineers who flush with pride no more. All have been consumed with relish and their bones bleach in the sun without. Stay away, I beg of you – but if duty calls then you must away to 214.'

171

You can't fight that thing – so use brains instead of brawn. Rush over to the door by which you entered, that's it. Stand there . . . wait for it . . . grab the handle. The tiglon charges . . . NOW! Turn to **213**.

172

Robbing Good sights along his arrow – aimed directly at your eye. What he sees is your arrow aimed directly at *his* eye. For some reason, he finds this slightly disconcerting. As do you as well, but you don't let on. The moment of tension stretches on and on until – with a sigh – he lowers his arrow. You do the same.

'You know – one of us could get killed this way. Usually I attack from ambush or pick on old ladies and that kind of thing.' He rubs his hand across his face and you can hear the harsh grating of the stubble on his chin. 'I got an idea. I don't want anyone to hear I was a weakling and let you get away with something, like you know. Now I'm a pretty good shot – the best in the jungle! – so what you say we have a shooting contest. If I lose I got to do you a favour, little chance of that ha-ha. If by a long shot and an accident you maybe win, why then I do you a favour. What do you say?'

What can you say? It looks like you have very little choice in the matter. You reluctantly mutter yes while the jungle ruffian marks a bullseye on each of two adjacent trees. He points and explains:

'We shoot at the same time – got that! The first one to get three bullseyes wins the match. So here we go!'

The match of the century starts. You raise your bow – he raises his – and you let fly at the same moment.

To discover the outcome of this battle of the ages you need your trusty APB again. Take it from pocket, flip it.

If it is heads thunk your arrow into **257**.

If tails, aim for **40**.

You slip the shield over your left arm, and seize the sword with your right hand. Are you ready? You had better be – because the door before you is grinding open, sunshine floods in. You straighten your back and march proudly to **144**.

Look, up ahead – a big tent with robots serving food. That must be the Soup Kitchen. That's it, get on the end of the line, you should be hungry by now. While you're waiting why don't you ask the nice man ahead of you where Groannsville is? If you ask him to go **101**, but if not go to **20** and get your soup.

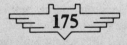

Won't you ever learn? Stay away from people on this planet. No good can ever come of meeting them. The guards simply grabbed you and threw you into this prison cell. You'll end up a slave for life if you don't get out of here.

That's it – dig through your pockets, you didn't bring all that expensive field agent equipment for nothing. No, not the horror comic, this is no time for reading. The guard will be here soon – he's unlocking the door now. Choose – quickly!

If it's a smoke bomb go to **64**.

If it's a gas bomb go to **29**.

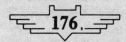

The road is endless and you are tired. You stagger and yawn and trudge on, until some time later you see **190** ahead and proceed to it.

Strong, isn't it! With one swipe of a paw it tore the sword from your grasp and knocked you across the room. It has bounced away – but it will charge again. You are doomed, unless you would like to hear my advice now. You would? Good. While there is still time flip quickly to **171**.

Walk carefully now, the planks are rotten. The river's far below and filled with rocks – don't look at it! That's better, you almost fell. Carry on. Good, almost over, a few feet more – WATCH IT!

Yes, the plank did break, and no, one shouldn't scream like that even when falling into the Rattlesnake River. Down and down you go and splash right into **205**.

A harsh blow to your head sends you sprawling. You awake, shaking your head dizzily, look up – and move aside just in time to avoid another blow from the vile fist of a horribly familiar and vile figure. It is Hairy Harry the Killer Cannibal! You turn to flee, but he seizes you in one hirsute paw and drags you back. He speaks:

'This is the end for you! Hand over the gold coins or I will eat you on the spot!'

He gapes hideously in your direction and a wave of cannibalistic halitosis washes over you and you see that his teeth are filed to sharp points. They clack in your direction, he pulls you to him, raises your forearm to bite out a chunk; you struggle helplessly to escape but cannot. Is this the end? It might be – what do you think? Don't curse at me – I didn't get you into this. You can ponder your fate for a while longer, or you can break the suspense by turning swiftly to **156**.

180

What a dusty road, but on you go, very strong of you. And there ahead is a giant building made of riveted steel. Doesn't look nice. No doors – but there is a telephone on the wall – with a sign next to it that reads: THE PRISON WARDEN MUST NOT BE BOTHERED. GO AWAY. Simple enough. If you want to go back to the crossroads at **97**, the old man may be back and he could tell you the way. Or if you feel bold, go to **46** and talk to the warden on the phone.

181

Phew, made it! Landed and skidded – but you didn't fall in. But you can't stay here very long. Look around, dash the perspiration from your eyes until you can see the layout. Two tiny crumbling ledges on the far side of the lava pool. What a choice – glad it is yours and not mine. So, before you fry – jump left to **204** or right to **122**.

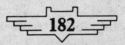

182

Running doesn't help for they are right behind you. Like a cornered beast you turn and the fight begins at **194**.

183

It worked – you are really fast on your feet. You jumped and the creature missed. But here it comes again and you have no choice but to jump again – this time jump to **112**.

184

What a shot! You got a bullseye and the battling bully missed completely. You are doing pretty well. Watch him sweat as you raise your bow again and let fly.

Let fly your coin as well. Heads gets you to **84**, tails to **27**.

185

Ouch! This guy is really rough. He knocks you to the ground where you lie, half-stunned. He steals your bow, your remaining arrows, roots through your pockets. The matter-transmitter doesn't interest him, but he takes everything else that you have. Including the seven gold coins.

And when he is all done, just to add insult to injury, he throws you over a nearby cliff and clanks off.

But you are not dead yet! You clutch at the roots that project from the cliff, hanging on for dear life, and only when the fiend has gone do you pull yourself back up with the last of your energy, right to **328**.

186

It's getting dark – looks like a storm coming up. Cold, rainy and spooky. Nice. What's that? Your feet are wet? How can your feet be wet already – and your legs too? I see now. The road is gone and you are up to your knees in mud. And sinking.

I have a feeling that you are in the dismal swamp. What do you do next?

If you scream wildly for help, go to **12**.

If you use your staff to push yourself clear, go to **33**.

187

Have you ever thought of going on the stage? No, I'm serious. With a lovely voice like yours, there is a great career in showbiz waiting for you.

In the future of course. Right now porcuswineology

heads the bill. The great beast skidded to a halt – splashing you with mud – and stared at you in amazement while you went through all sixteen verses of *Colonel Bogey*. I think it blushed at some of the lyrics – who would have thought that you could shame a porcuswine!

In any case, when you had finished with that the two of you sang the duet from *Così fan Piggi*, as well as a heartwarming rendition of *Does your Mother come from Pigland* and a rousing chorus of *I'm a Porcuswine and I'm OK*. Quieter now it sits and fixes you with one porky eye and speaks.

'You know, for a squishy human being, you got a pretty good voice. Of course you will never obtain the depth of emotion or feeling of a porcuswine – but we can't all be perfect. But I gotta move on, I heard the crashing of a tyrannosaurus rex in the jungle and I'm *dying* to eat one of those mothers. Now you wouldn't be rattling around this dangerous forest without a reason. And I bet that I can guess what it is. You're after the Jewel of the Jungle, aren't you? Well, there is only one way to get there since the bridge fell down. You gotta fly. Just follow this path until you come to the Roc. Biggest bird in the world – and the oldest. It's called the Roc of Ages. It will carry you there – but only if you feed it. There is fruit growing along the path. Pick an armload and take it along as a bribe.

'So long, kid, see you in the chorus!'

With these words the monster crashes off through the jungle leaving you on your own once again. You have had good luck with porcuswine, big, evil and foul-smelling as they are, so you take this porky pincushion's word about the Roc and walk off to **104**.

A dusty, ancient hall stretches out ahead of you. Eerie green light filters down from cracks in the walls, rats and other obnoxious things scuttle away as you approach. Not nice. Yes, draw your sword, good idea, and walk carefully down the hall. It turns and twists, then ends in a staircase. You have no choice – you must go down. Carefully, one step at a time. To the bottom where there are two doors.

That's encouraging – you must be in the right tower for the door on the left has a sign on it that reads: THIS WAY TO THE PRICELESS JEWEL OF THE JUNGLE.

Good, go that way – no? Oh, you want to read what it says on the other door. Nothing important, really. Just one of those empty threats. ENTER HERE AND DIE INSTANTLY FOR A GRUESOME DEATH AWAITS YOU!

I agree – you do have a problem. Death or jewels. Which one? And are the signs lying? Only one answer, you must use that scientific prognosticating device the APB. You can safely leave the choice to science. That's it, flip it high.

Heads you go left to **267**.

Tails, proceed right to **150**.

Well, some days nothing seems to go right. You grabbed the gas bomb all right – but Betsy is a fast girl and seized it and hurled it away. But you were fast too – oh, boy! – and you took the chance to throw a smokebomb too. But, unhappily, because of your chains you couldn't escape in the darkness – and Betsy gave you a black eye for your trouble. You're still on your way to Groannsville. But – look – there is someone else approaching!

What an ugly bloke! Fists like hams, eyes like yams, hair like a lamb's! He may sound edible, but he is still nasty. He's running this way now, waving a club. Betsy is squaring off in a karate fighting stance.

There is going to be a battle. They look evenly matched. Say – if you help one of them win you may get out of this fix. So do something!

If you help Betsy, turn to **94**.

If you help the thug, turn to **65**.

190

You are in trouble, for as you walk you become aware of footsteps on the pavement behind you. Knowing this can mean no good you walk faster. This proves to be a good idea until you also hear footsteps on the road ahead. Before you can dart into the trees the thugs appear behind you and in front of you.

You have very little choice at this time. You can run into the woods to **182** in the hope that you can escape them. Or you can stay and fight on **194**.

191

Another crawl, but this seems shorter. Long before terminal exhaustion sets in you see a light ahead. You crawl faster and emerge into a solid steel chamber with riveted walls. And no exit that you can find. It might be wisest to go back into the tunnel – but, no! – with a hideous crunching sound, the tunnel collapses. You just got out in time. But now what? Is there something in that dark corner of the chamber? You go forward to see. Yes – there is a bright red handle protruding from the wall with a tasteful skull capping its end. Doesn't look too promising. There is something carved into the metal above the handle. Instructions in thirty-four languages, half of them long vanished. It can be translated to mean – sorry, I didn't know that you could read any of them. I agree. The simplest translation would be PULL ME. Do you have a choice?

After brooding a bit you reach out quivering fingers and pull –

The floor opens. You are falling, falling down to **98**.

192

Quiet as a mouse you creep, holding your breath, wishing that you still had the ironbound club with you. But that is long gone. All you have now are your guts, your strength – and all the other items in your pockets.

Something stirs – you stop! It was nothing, just the wind flapping the fabric of the balloon. You go forward again and there before you, you see . . .

A rather undramatic row of footprints in the sand. The professor has gone. You have no other choice – you must follow him to **225**.

193

What's that ahead? If mine eyes don't deceive me, there is a walled city coming up ahead. And if you listen closely you can hear a distant groaning. This could only be Groannsville. That wall will be difficult to climb – but you could always go in through the front gate. What about the armed guards there? You might very well ask – what *about* them? It's your decision – I'm just along for the ride.

If you want to take a chance on the gate, go to **175**.

Or climb the wall at **86**.

194

Strong as you are, brave as you are – and tired as you are – the outcome is not in doubt. They swarm all over you and batter you to the ground. When your head stops reeling, you realize that your hands are tied behind your back. What a predicament. Surrounded by rough thugs and guttural oaths, you are off to **334**.

195

You never learn – do you? The nice young lad punched you up when you talked to him and you just managed to escape. But you were tired and took a rest – then fell asleep. You're awake now and look up – and horror of horrors look who is there!

Do you recognize that great build and wild laughter? I thought you might. It's Betsy Booster – and she has caught you again.

So, kicking and screaming, you are dragged once more to **65**. But you are in luck – Arbuthnot is there as well. *This* time you should know what to do!

196

My, but you *are* strong. You won the fight easily with a one-two knockout punch. Slow down, something around the bend – yes indeed. Can it be? It must be. The shining white walls of Crapper's Castle. The gate yawns wide, beckoning. But you shake your head no. You have learned your lessons well. Wait until dark, then scale the wall and turn to **153**.

197

The empty hall stretches out ahead of you, there are running footsteps. You run yourself, right to 242.

198

That was rough – but you did it and I am proud of you. Don't curse – I heard that! And don't mutter about some doing all the work and others doing all the talking. Good, joke a bit, it will help you dry off. Trot around the bend – ooops! Yes, he does look tough – but you are tough too! Time for your Amphisbenic Bipolar Determinator, or APB as it is called for short – or coin as you insist on calling it. Heads you go to **28**, or tails to **196**.

199

What a wild ride! The great wings flap and you are up and out and over the jungle, hurtling through the air. Giant thunderclouds pile up ahead and the Roc of Ages croaks powerfully:

'**Thunderstorms! I laugh at thunderstorms – here we go!**'

With a cry of rage the batty buzzard dives straight into the storm. In an instant you are tossed by high winds, gasping for air as the rain pelts you. All you can do is grab tight to the bird's feathers and hope that this is not the time of year that Rocs moult. Lightning blasts close by, blinding you, deafening you with the roll of thunder. There is a cry of avian pain as the lightning sets some of the Roc's feathers on fire. Wow, they stink! But the rain puts the fire out. Even the Roc has had enough of this and it dives out of the storm and floats on giant wings over the jungle:

'Where did you say that you were going, oh puny one? I can't seem to remember . . . I'm getting sleepy for some unknown reason. Wait – I remember now. You want the ruined castle so you can steal the Jewel of the Jungle just one more time. You humans break me up with your wanton love of baubles. Give me an ox or a kangarabbit any time.'

The tremendous bird dives, then straightens out and points to the jungle below with one wingtip.

'Look down, miserable mite – and beware. The ruins are below. See where two towers emerge from the jungle. Descend the correct tower and you will find the Jewel of the Jungle. Descend the wrong one and you will only encounter a horrible death. The correct tower is . . .'

Why does it break off speaking at this vital point? How should I know? – but it does. Then it roars with rage:

'Sleepy . . . Listen, you midget moron – did you pick that fruit from the Grove of Academe? If you picked the wrong colour fruit, it will act as a strong sleeping drug. And I . . . have the feeling . . . that I noshed the wrong one . . .'

In mid-word it has fallen asleep and begins to snore loudly. But apparently it is used to sleeping on the wing for it soars on. But it is not flapping – just gliding. I have a suggestion. Try pushing its head to one side and see what happens. Great – it turns in the direction that you pushed. So you can do it. You can guide the Roc so that it lands on the correct tower and you will get the Jewel and everything will be OK.

How do I know which is the right tower? This whole ballgame is new to me. Please don't waste time cursing like that – we are getting lower all the time. If I were you I would flip the APB coin and decide – you have just enough time!

If it is heads swing the sleeping bird towards the left-hand tower and when it comes close jump at once to **117**.

If tails point the Roc at the right-hand tower and get ready to jump to **327**!

Enough is enough yet already! The signs have all been changed about. You should have gone to **53** – so don't waste time – get there now!

'**I start off easy,**' the Star Beast belches forth. '**Now the big one. What is black and deadly and sits in a tree?**'

When you think you know the answer turn to **85**.

You are at the bottom of an immense pit that stretches up and up until the sky is just a tiny patch above. But you cannot climb the smooth walls. Nor would you want to! The pit is filled with giant birds – and one is now diving on you its great serrated beak open to munch you to death, its foul breath washing over you like the exhaust of a millennia-old sewer. You quickly decide between the doorway to the east, go to **226**, or the one to the south, go to **210**.

203

Is it still a millennia-old illusion that you are about to escape? Does real sunshine really lurk outside the exit to the north – then go to **208**? Or should you not risk it and go south to **264**.

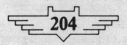

204

Like a bird you soar – up, up and away! And land with a crashing thud on the ledge which begins to break away from the rock wall behind it . . .

You really do move quite fast when you want to. Leaping, scrambling – and cursing when a drop of lava lands sizzling on your leg – you dance along the collapsing rock towards a gaping tunnel entrance and simply hurl yourself to **333**.

205

It's a good thing that you can swim. No, don't panic! It's just a swimming rattlesnake. And there's another one. Who do you think they named the river after? You *are* a fast swimmer, aren't you! Particularly when competing in the race with snakes. Going to go ashore? Yes, but where? A nice little beach there, but hooligans could be hiding in the shrubs. You might be better off landing on the rocks. Difficult and dangerous – but no shrubs. Turn to **3** for the beach – or **198** for the rocks.

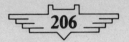

206

Hard work, but you can do it: stumble along the trail – but don't stumble off the edge . . .

It's one of those days. You fall – all the way to **107**.

207

Stop sticking your little finger into your ear like that and shaking your head back and forth. I hear it too – there is nothing wrong with your ears. Yes, correct, right – the repulsively ugly creature is singing. Singing in a lovely soprano voice – and singing a love song. And, by George, I recognize the tune – I bet you do too. Hear, listen closely:

> *Mud, mud, glorious mud,*
> *Nothing quite like it to muffle a thud.*
> *So come with me quickly,*
> *Into the mud thickly,*
> *And there we will wallow*
>   *In glorious mud . . .*

Very nice I suppose, particularly if you are another porcuswine. So what are you going to do? Step forward with your sword raised and frighten the creature out of the way? All right, if you think that is best march nobly to **224**. But it is really a rough-looking brute. I would suggest, only a suggestion, mind you – you can stop laughing – that you sing a duet with the thing. It really is a music lover and it might appreciate a little harmonizing. Can't find too much of that in the swamp, can it? Yes, I see you rolling on the ground and holding your sides, very repellent it is too. So go fight the thing – at **224** – unless you would like to sing along with swiney at **266**.

208

Oh what a persevering devil you are! You crawl through a crack in the crumbling wall and are outside the ruins at last. Behind you there is a rumbling crunch as all of the ceilings fall in – and about time too. You turn your back on the now vanished millennia-old ruin and follow the running footsteps of your quarry, the mad prof. Follow them all the way to **261**.

209

You *are* lucky! You have been spared – the delicate little thumb of Sadie the Sadistic points skyward. Slobber a bit of thanks to her then go at once to **335**.

210

Well we all – even I, but very rarely – make mistakes. This is not a room but only a small niche in the wall. Outside, in **202** to the north, the evil bird screams and awaits your return. Take a deep breath – ready, steady – GO!

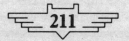

211

Goodness, what strange animals there are on all the walls. Coloured, apparently in motion due to an ancient millennia-lost science. As you walk they appear to run, walk, sit, eat, snap and other interesting things. But you will not be distracted! You push on until you determine that the animal room has three exits. To the north to **297**; west to **241** or east to **281**.

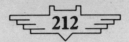

212

No light, no nothing. No gravity either since you keep bumping against the ceiling. Go on – for it would be death to stop now. Go on in the darkness until your groping fingers discover that you can go north to **240** or south to **296**.

213

You open the door and step aside. Tons of thundering rocks tumble and roar in and bury the tiglon. Only its tail protrudes from the mountain of rubble. This twitches once – then is still. What a killer you are! Swaggering, you slip your sword back into the scabbard, stroll across the chamber – then open the door there and step through to **188**.

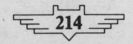

214

You are on the road again, having eaten and drunk well, and following instructions you are on the lookout for the hanging bridge across Death Valley. In its noisome depths runs the poisonous Rattlesnake River. There it is ahead – but, oh, horrors – the planks are decayed and broken and might break under your weight. But see, there is a path to the river's bank, where a boatman awaits. If you decide on the boat turn to **26** – or turn to **178** if you wish to chance the bridge.

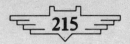

215

'Thank you oh mighty and lenient stranger! As a reward for your justice I will tell you what you need to know. When you cross the bridge you will come to a fork in the trail. If you go left you will die within seconds, killed by the poisonous snakes that abound there. Take the right fork to safety. Now go – with a poor man's thanks.'

Nodding acceptance of what is your due you stride across the bridge to **128**.

216

Horrors! A great brute with a club – it can only be Sluj the Slaver, and besides that, look at that row of chained slaves. I remember when he was sent to this prison planet for crimes too hideous to mention. He is beating that guy on the ground. But look, that is no ordinary guy! There could not be two faces in the galaxy as ugly as that. It is Arbuthnot the Rejected who befriended you. Friendship demands that you turn to **44**.

217

Yes, I think that this hideous chamber was a mistake too. Hot and smoky and smelling of evil and noxious fumes, you stagger on and on – to discover that the only way out is to the west to **281**.

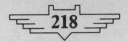

218

Thugs. Lots of them. They beat down your feeble resistance, you should have listened to me, and a club silences the curses on your lips, you shouldn't refer to your superiors that way, and as you sink into unconsciousness you turn to **28**.

219

Look, recruit, I like you. I really do. Take some more of the mud out of your ear so you can hear me. Go fight that prickly porker if you think that is best. I'll close my eyes because I hate to see one so young die so horribly. So instead of dying, why not reconsider the duet, clear your throat, hum a few bars of *Land of Hope and Glory* and proceed musically to **266**.

220

Simply amazing what those millennia-dead scientists could do. You *know* that you are underground – yet you could be in a rock-rimmed meadow with white clouds above and soft blue grass beneath your feet. Yes, blue, you have not suddenly gone colourblind. Maybe they liked grass that way. In any case you wander on, smiling and happy, reluctant to leave this sunny millennia-dead paradise: through the portal to the west to **240**, or through the one to the north to **235**, or perhaps to the south to **234**.

221

Tastes good. The prof is obviously full of crap. You finish this, and the coconut as well, and turn back to the dragon at **299**.

222

Pitch black, up to your neck in cold water – while the spirits of millennia-dead creatures nuzzle your legs under the surface. Yes, you certainly have been in better places. You follow the sound of pouring water to **228** to the east or **235** to the south.

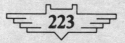

223

Feel better for that? Fate calls. Move it to **96**.

224

Wow – talk about fast! That fat old porcuswine charged you, without missing a note, knocked your legs out from under you and sent you aspirin over applecart into the mud. Grope for your sword because here it comes again. No more singing – but ohh, the horrible grunting! Like a runaway steam locomotive. Your sword will never penetrate those steely quills. Quick, dodge that way to **219**.

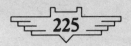

You are tired but you press on, never losing sight of the footsteps. They go straight to the horizon, then over the horizon, and when you follow them some more you discover that they lead straight to an immense portal in the wall of a giant, ancient building. It does not look nice at all for it is covered with obscene carvings and hideous monster representations, countless numbers of them stretching out to each side as far as the eye can see. And the footsteps go straight into the opening . . . why did you stop walking?

Ahh, I see, a message carved in letters thirty centimetres high in the wall beside the entrance. Most interesting. What do you mean that you can't read it? It is in Esperanto, a language spoken by everyone, see '*Vi alvenas je la pordo de la teruro de* . . .' No, I'm not showing off. When this mission is over you are ordered to learn Esperanto at once.

It reads, in translation, of course: YOU HAVE ARRIVED AT THE GATE OF THE FRIGHTFUL, OF THE PRISON OF THE MONSTROUS STAR BEAST. BE WARNED. TO ENTER HERE MEANS CERTAIN DEATH. WE, THE ANCIENT RACE OF KAKALOKS, HAVE BUILT THIS PRISON TO SAVE THE GALAXY FROM THIS CREATURE. AND LITTLE THANKS WE GOT BECAUSE BUILDING THIS BANKRUPTED OUR ANCIENT RACE AND WE ARE NOW ALL DEAD SO THE HELL WITH YOU ANYWAY.

You are impressed by this, as well you might be, and you're instantly faced with the realization that you must follow the prof into this place. You have the choice of turning at once to **96**, or of taking a little rest first at **223**.

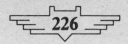

226

A small and dark chamber no bigger than a box. You have to push your way into it. You can touch the three exits with your outstretched hands. The one to the north leads to **294**; the one to the west to **202**, and the one to the east to **296**.

227

Great pillars hold up the ceiling. But they are crumbled and old and at the sound of your footsteps dust rains down and pieces flake off. You hurry on, trembling with fear lest the roof drop before you pass through this chamber of despair. There is an exit behind you to the north that leads to **253**, or one to the east that goes to **297**.

228

We all make mistakes. The water has tumbled you around and around in here, numbing your brain, or what is left of it, until you discover the only way out is to the west back to **222**.

229

All of this has bored the Star Beast and it has fallen sound asleep and is snoring out clouds of smoke. You also note that Prof. Geisteskrank was only feigning sleep on his part and he had really been working to open his cage and has done so and has escaped through the door marked EXIT.

If you rush after him go to **35**. Or if you proceed with trepidation to **197**.

You run! And I don't blame you. Crashing through the undergrowth, around the trees, up the hills and down the dales until you stream with sweat. You stagger into the shade of a large tree, panting for breath, turn and look –

And there is the hideous creature just behind you!

No chance to think. Nock arrow, draw bow – and shoot as it charges and its foul breath washes over you.

Zip now to **88** to see if you are still alive.

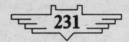

Attack! Oh you are a reckless one. Straight at the gun. Too late – his trigger finger tightens and he cackles one last cackle as the cloud of gas bursts against your face. You fall into dizzy darkness on **82**.

Well done. He rushes past you and you give him a swipe on the back of the head as he goes by. He falls – but springs to his feet again and advances. This time it is you who attack, screaming horribly, aiming a great blow that he cannot dodge. Your sword descends – and you find out what happens at **81**.

233

You *are* lucky! You have been spared – the delicate little thumb of Sadie the Sadistic points skyward. Slobber a bit of thanks to her then go at once to **335**.

234

This must have been their power-generating chamber for it is of giant size and filled with the hulking bulks of millennia-dead machines. You stagger on, hour after hour, wanting to stop but knowing that you dare not for that would be certain death. But you manage to keep track of your wanderings among the machines and finally figure out that there are only two exits from this place. **220** to the north and **241** to the west.

235

Hurry, run – cover your eyes with your hands to guard against the sand blowing in the hot wind. This place is horrible. It is only by touch that you determine that you have to go either north to **222** or south to **220**. Make up your mind quickly!

236

Ugggh! Too disgusting! Go back at once to whence you came!

237

Not too good! He dodges your sword and leaps forward, dagger swishing. You dodge – but not quickly enough. The hilt catches you on the side of the helmet, stunning you, you fall – fall all the way to **79**.

238

Can this be the end? You are trapped in a strange and hideous substance that clings and cloys like the deadly fingers of a long-lost love . . . Yes, all right, I'll save the saccharine similes for another time. I can only look on at your silent struggle as you manage to reach the only exit to the north at **208**.

239

You are in a room with two doors leading from it and you hear the roar of the crowd from the arena behind. An old man stands quavering before you – hark, for he speaks:

'You who are about to die I salute you. It is a noble thing to die for the Sons of Sadism. I would do it myself but I am not feeling very noble today. You will have noticed that one of these doors has LIONS written on it, while the other is inscribed WOLVES. The choice is yours – you may pick either one. Why do you laugh so hysterically, young warrior? Oh, you don't think much of going into the arena empty-handed. Well here is the only weapon that I have and it is yours.'

From under his patched and filthy robe, he takes a large feather and hands it to you. And you take it – too shocked to do otherwise. You examine the feather – but it is just a feather. When you look up, the oldster is gone.

Well, no point in hanging about here. If it is LIONS that you choose, why, then proceed nobly to **24**. Or if it is wolves march forward to **318**.

You are absolutely right! Through some miracle of mis-applied millennia-old science the iron floor to this metal chamber is glowing red-hot. So before the soles of your shoes burn through hurry east to **220** or south to **212**.

This must have been the aliens' cold-storage locker for it is cold and dark and filled with large and frozen forms. Could this be the frozen meat for their alien din-dins, kept safe here for millennia? You are not hungry enough or warm enough to find out – and besides, how do you go about eating something the size of a tyrannosaurus? Your feet frozen, your hands so numb they are unto blocks of ice, you carry on until you determine that the exit on the west goes to **234**, to the east to **211**, the one to the south to **238**.

You hurry out of this last tunnel into the blessed sun once more, the murky and dangerous lair of the Star Beast behind you at last. And your quarry has not yet escaped you for you see his footsteps proceeding ahead of you across the sand. You follow them, keeping on your guard, to **8**.

243

You *are* lucky! You have been spared – the delicate little thumb of Sadie the Sadistic points skyward. Slobber a bit of thanks to her then go at once to **335**.

244

The floor here is as soft as down. You are tired, you need rest – but you dare not. You hurry on to **259** to the north or **295** to the east.

245

The trail goes on and on. It is getting along towards evening and you are very tired. Should you rest here – or carry on? Problems, problems. But, yes, I heard it too. The sound of running water ahead. Curious, you investigate. Carefully though, creeping through the underbrush and peering out at the scene ahead.

The path drops down to the brink of a narrow chasm, with the bubbling river far below. It will be easy enough to cross, for a fine stone bridge spans the gap.

Great – except for the fact that a burly guard in heavy armour and armed with an iron club stands at this end of the bridge. To cross the bridge you must pass him. But you are tired. Maybe it might be best to wait until morning when you are fresher? After you have finished the last of the wine.

Or should you grasp the nettle and go on? In the morning there might be more guards here and you will never get across.

If you decide to get it over with now gird up your loins and march forth to **6**. Or if you want to rest first and go at it fresh in the light of dawn, then yawn and proceed to **127**.

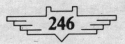

Well done! You have cut the robot's club in half with your sharp blade. He retreats, cursing harsh mechanical robotic curses – then draws a hammer. Then attacks again. You step back out of reach and aim a blow at his legs at **258**. Or if you swing at his head, go to **262**.

Wow! What a relief after the molasses room. A long and cushioned corridor down which you gallop. Around the bends and through the turns, downhill, faster and faster – ohh what happiness! Until you crash into the end of the tunnel. I would sob like a babe as well. There is no way out! Other than back up the corridor to the west to the horrors of **296** the molasses room . . .

You reach for the crown – then stop. Yes, I see it too, a thin wire runs from the crown down through a hole in the table. If you pick up the crown, the wire gets pulled – and something decidedly nasty is sure to happen.

That's it – be wary and stay alive. Step back, extend your sword at arm's length – and pick up the crown on **165**.

249

Back out of sight you slink, under the heavy leaves and vines, out of sight of the trail. The footsteps come closer – then stop. There is a hmm-hmming sound. Then a harsh voice speaks:

'I am a master of the jungle lore and it is easy for me to see that someone else has passed here within the last thirty-seven seconds, has paused, has spit into the forest, then slunk into hiding. Step forward, varlet, for I know that you lurk there!'

Not much choice is there? Stop lurking and step forward to **131**.

250

It roars mechanical roars of victory, thinking that it has you now, leaps forward. But you are a fighting devil, you are! As it jumps you lash out with your legs and send the thing sprawling and falling – right back to the edge of the chasm at **316**!

251

You are in a dark room lit only by the feeble light of a guttering candle. It is hot, close, oppressive, claustrophobic – stop pulling at the door, it is no use for it locked behind you. Is there no other way out? Investigate, that's the old Special Corps way! No windows, that's obvious – and no doors. Bit of a dilemma this. Yes, I do appreciate your position. No food, no water, no future. Don't just sit on the stone floor and be depressed. Keep trying.

You have noticed something! I can tell by the way you jump to your feet and rush to the wall, to a barely visible niche there. A handle! Pull it and a secret panel is sure to open, just like in the bad TV films! No, I didn't notice the sign under the handle. I do now. It reads: DO NOT PULL THIS HANDLE!

That is *very* interesting. Quite an intellectual problem – not to say one of survival.

How long do I think you have been in this room now? Well, looking at the candle which is almost out, I would say it's been about three hours. Yes, the time has arrived to do something. Yes, I stand corrected, not some-thing but one-thing, the only thing that you can do.

Pull the handle.

You stand, walk slowly towards it. Seize it. Brace yourself – and pull!

A trapdoor opens under your feet and, helpless once again, you fall directly to **239**.

252

'Stop!' the robot commands in a rusty voice. **'Who goes there?'**

'Me,' you respond, with very little imagination.

'Advance, Me, and give the password.'

You move forward slowly and attempt a ruse:

'The password is antidisestablishmentarianism.'

It's a good ruse – but not good enough. Swinging its club, the robot jumps forward shouting: **'You're a spy – that's yesterday's password!'**

If you step aside to dodge the blow go to **74**. Or, if you counter his blow with your sword go to **246**.

You drop and land on a heap of sand which has sifted down through the ruined ceiling. But you are trapped down here – the hole above is too high up for you to reach. And the prof has gone before you – his footsteps lead across the piled sand to the bare floor beyond. There are strange alien devices carved into the walls, still sharp and clear and glowing with a lambent light even after all the millennia that have passed. You have no choice, you must go on. There are two doors leading from the chamber, one to the east and one to the south. You examine the hard material of the floor carefully – but there is no sign which way your quarry went. You must decide.

Another thing, and this isn't important really, just a suggestion that will save your life. Now listen, why don't you grub out that bit of pencil you always carry. And a scrap of paper. Good. Now, as you go, make a little floor plan. In case you have gone wrong you can always retrace your steps. Then, eventually, you can find the exit – *if* there is an exit of course.

If you reluctantly decide to go east go to **269**. Or, if with equal reluctance you go south, then go to **227**.

Bullseye! Wow! What an eye. Keep up the good work. Draw and shoot. Shoot to **27** with a heads, to **163** with tails.

255

Made it! You are safe on the rooftop and pelting after the prof, waving your club over your head and crowing with victory. He stumbles and falls! He is yours! You will grab him now and save the galaxy and take him to prison and go home and have a hot bath and all kinds of nice things like that . . .

Except that he is sitting up and pointing a large and evil-looking gun at you. He speaks:

'**Advance vun step more und I vill pull der trigger and that will be end of you, dummerkopf!**'

Quite a position to be in. If you attack in any case go to **231**. If you hesitate turn to **10**.

256

Quiet as a mouse you creep, holding your breath, wishing that you still had the ironbound club with you. But that is long gone. All you have now are your guts, your strength, and all the other items in your pockets.

Something stirs – you stop! Nothing, just the wind flapping the fabric of the balloon. You go forward again and there before you, you see . . .

A rather undramatic row of footprints in the sand. The professor has gone. You have no other choice – you must follow him to **225**.

257

What a shot! You got a bullseye and the battling bully missed completely. You are doing pretty good. Watch him sweat as you raise your bows again and let fly.

Let fly your coin as well. Heads gets you to **84**, tails to **27**.

258

Not too good! He jumps over your sword and leaps forward, hammer swishing. You dodge – but not quickly enough. The head of the hammer catches you on the side of the helmet, stunning you, and you fall – fall all the way to **250**.

259

Trapped like a rat! Stop saying 'eeeek' over and over and draw yourself together. You can still go back by the door to the south that leads to **244**.

260

This is some trail and after following it for a while you begin to doubt if that green-clad ruffian was telling you the truth. The trail goes on and on without end. It is easy enough to follow because is has been marked with spatters of some red substance on the trees and rocks along the way. Can that red substance be blood? Best not to ask.

Not only is the trail marked with red – but there are cheerful signs all along the way like: STILL WALKING? I

THOUGHT YOU WOULD BE DEAD BY NOW. And even more heartening ones like: DANGER – MANEATING SPIDERS! and: I HOPE YOU SIGNED YOUR WILL! Pretty strong stuff – but you are a pretty strong recruit. You may stagger, but you carry on. Never tiring – well, yes, tiring once in a while. Sure, sit down, and take a little break. No harm in that . . .

Wow! I never saw anyone leap into the air that high so quickly. Yes, I would probably leap too if sharp teeth had emerged from the mud right under my fundament and bitten out a bit of flesh. Sorry. When I said there was no harm sitting down I had *no* idea that you would be sitting down right on top of a hideous mud-snapper. Time to go on in any case.

Gloomy swamp. The cries of deadly creatures on all sides. Poisonous moss draping the boughs. And from ahead on the path hideous cries of pain – abruptly terminated by crunching as of great jaws eating flesh and bone . . .

No, you can't run away like that. Whatever is ahead must be faced – or you will spend the rest of what will undoubtedly be a very short life on this planet. Don't grate your teeth like that, it makes an awful sound.

Mind made up? Good. Advance slowly towards the sound, part the leaves and look . . .

You're right – that is a repellent sight. A giant porcu-swine, twice as big as the first one that you encountered, is munching on the remains of a brontosaurus. What an appetite! The last thing you want to do is face up to this creature. You begin to withdraw – but it is too late! The vile porcuswine sniffs the air and bellows. It has detected your smell! It hurls aside the goggy remains of the bronto-saurus and charges in your direction. What do you do? Don't ask me – this is your adventure. All right then, I can give you *some* help. I can help you list the possibilities:

You still have your invisibility belt. If you want to use that press the buckle and go invisibly to **312**.

Or if you want to run away from the beast run at once to **287**.

Or, yes, I hadn't thought of that. You had such good luck in the arena, showing your mastery of the lower orders of beast, that you might want to try it again. If you do, why, then stand your ground and look the hideous porcuswine sternly in its bloodshot eye until it is humbled and stops on **141**.

Or, laughable idea, you just might want to sing a little duet with it. Which is OK as long as your friends never find out that you sing romantic songs with 6 tonne porcuswine. If this is your not-too-bright choice, then hum along to **187**.

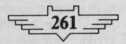

The prof's footsteps lead over a hill and on to a paved road beyond. But which way did he go? There is no one here to ask and no way for you to tell. So now is the time to use that complicated technical device the amphisbenic bipolar determinator, the wondrous APB. Or coin, as you insist on calling it. Flip it, watch it . . . it's standing on edge. Better try again. Great. If it is heads go to **227**. Or if it's tails, to **290**.

Not too good! It dodges your sword and leaps forward, hammer swishing. You dodge – but not quickly enough. The head of the hammer catches you on the side of the helmet, stunning you, you fall – fall all the way to **250**.

263

With your last strength you haul yourself up from the water by climbing the vines and sprawl on the grass above. Your head swims and fatigue clutches you – but you are young, strong and healthy and the effects of the cheap wine have worn off. Strength returned, you climb to your feet and turn and . . .

Find yourself staring at an incredibly evil-looking creature with eyes the size of soup plates, teeth like daggers, tentacles like ropes – and terminal halitosis. You don't know what it is? Unhappily I do. Yes, I'll tell you, just don't screech like that. It is the rare and deadly Green Pippick Monster – see the green pippick on its extended and gross belly? Very poisonous. You must try to kill it with a well-placed arrow – or flee before it attacks.

That's it, slip your hand into your pocket and take out your APB. Also called a coin. My goodness, it's getting rusty, what are they making coins out of these days! That's it, flip it silently and look at it.

If it is heads, go quickly to **272**.

If tails, slip in silence to **280**.

264

Yes, it is hard to think with the driving rain, rolling thunder and crashing lightning – all undoubtedly generated by a millennia-old machine for some incredibly millennia-old stupid reason. But with the flashes of lightning you make out the even darker mouths of the exits. One to the east to **294**, the other to the north to **203**. You leave.

SPLASH!

Down and down you go, round and round you go. Tossed by the water, deeper and ever deeper. Then you begin the long swim upward, holding your breath, your lungs bursting, daring not to breathe or you will fill your aching lungs with water and will certainly drown.

But you must breathe!

But you must wait! You cannot – you gasp in . . .

AIR! For you have reached the surface. You are happy to drift along getting your strength back, drifting with the current. At last you feel better and you kick towards shore. But where should you land? There is a sandbar there where you can climb out of the water and rest before tackling the hidden dangers of juicy jungle.

Or you can swim to those vines and pull yourself up into the protection of the trees. But nasties could be hiding there. However if you come ashore on the sandbar whatever is lurking in the undergrowth could see you and sneak up and attack.

What to do? Sorry, I'm of no help at all. I've never seen this stretch of country before. The decision is yours. If it is the sandbar swim lustily to 135.

Or splash to 263 for the vines.

Now wasn't that nice? After a friendly chorus of *Going My Way* and a rousing stanza or two of *Old MacDonald Had a Farm* and a melodious rendering of *This Little Piggy Went to Market* you two have become stout chums. Look! Is that a tear in one porcine eye? I do believe that it is! You have a good mate here. Listen as it rattles its quills, then speaks:

'Welcome to the wallow, oh melodious stranger. I haven't had a good sing-song like that since I was a pincushiony-piglet. My dear mother, now departed this vale of tears, taught me to sing. She always told us when we wallowed in the wallow that she had not been born a porcuswine but instead had once been human. Would you believe that? She had been a mezzosoprano and had sung with La Scala. Until at a famous début she had failed to hit C above High C and the conductor, who was a bit of a demonologist in his spare time, turned her into a porcuswine. She got hers back because she tromped him to death and ate him right then and there, then escaped through the orchestra pit. You believe that, don't you?'

Good, good, nod your head like a fool. Never argue with a nutty four-tonne porcuswine.

'You do believe it? How sweet. I don't. I think she was just another spiky porker with delusions of grandeur. But there you are. None of us are perfect. Been nice to sing with you – do stop for a duet any time you are in the jungle. The path goes thataway, right to 73.'

The sign must have been right because no instant death grabs you – nor a lingering death either. More steps, more musty smells and scratching of fleeing and unseen rats. Another door ahead, just enough light from the cracks in the walls to read what is painted there.

THE JOOL ROOM – KEEP OUT!

Right, they can't spell very well, but maybe they are

better jewellers. Throw the door open and leap through to
119.

You can't do it – you're an old softy you are! For as you
walk away you hear the ugly laughter of the brute in
human form as he lays into the robots with a whip. They
scream and he laughs the louder. And you think of all the
friendly felines that will be turned into cat pudding if you
don't stop this monster once and for all and you wheel
about, roaring with anger, and charge to **157**.

Do you see what is carved on that wall! What filthy pigs
these creatures were!! That's right, avert your eyes, there
are some things best not looked at. Look around the room
instead. The door behind you leads to the west, and
another, in front of you, leads to the east. If you go west
turn to **253**, or if east turn to **293**.

There is the stamping of mighty feet ahead of you on the
trail. Before you can find a hiding place a hairy brute with
a great club springs out at you. He is too big to fight,
believe me! No one will call you a coward for running from
a creature like that. He can't be too fleet of foot. Turn and
take off!

Right to **75**.

It's a little difficult hanging by one hand and wriggling out of your chainmail. Not only difficult – you quickly discover that it cannot be done. You discard your helmet easily enough. But what next? Hey – that's *very* good! You hang your bow and arrows from the ladder. Then turn upside down, hook your toes over a rung – and zip! the chainmail is gone. You get big marks for that one.

Yes, it is almost time. Nothing much more can be accomplished hanging around this ladder. So, after tying your bow and arrows firmly in place, you take breath after deep breath filling your lungs and your blood with fresh, nourishing oxygen. Let go with one hand . . .

Correct. You'll have to let go with the other hand too if you are going to fall into that cold-looking, nasty, fast-flowing river. I am encouraging, aren't I!

Muttering one last profanity you let go . . .

And fall all the way to **265**.

You have wisely decided to shoot the filthy thing – and I don't blame you! With careful motions you slot an arrow to the string . . . draw back the bow –

It attacks! You let fly! Your arrow zings out and, to discover what has happened you zing to **88**.

273

Here you are in a dusty room with four doors on the far wall numbered, as even you can see, with the numbers one, two, three and four. Behind you a sickeningly familiar voice booms out:

'**Choose now, you swinish slaves, choose your destiny! Pick a door and enter it and see how lucky you have been! But you cannot enter door four until you have fought two times in the arena and have survived. So choose between the other three!**'

Well don't ask me – I don't know where the doors lead to any more than you do. The instructions seem simple enough: if you like door one then proceed to **285**. Or if door two meets your fancy you will go to **239**. However, if you think that door three is the winner go laughing to **251**. Which leaves your only other choice – door four which you cannot enter now.

274

You *are* lucky! You have been spared – the delicate little thumb of Sadie the Sadistic points skyward. Slobber a bit of thanks to her then go at once to **335**.

275

You run for it knowing that these robots are a worthless lot and will do nothing to help you. You are right too, for they are fleeing in all directions crying out with fear. The brute with the club stumbles over them, but comes after you. For a thing that size he is pretty fast. You are never going to outrun him. You turn to fight but it is too late. A great, hairy, unwashed hand seizes you up. You are helpless in the powerful grasp. You writhe but cannot escape as the brute paws through your clothing and finds the Jewel of the Jungle. Roaring with happiness, it ties you up with vines stripped from the trees.

This is not too good. If you want to find out what happens next you'll have to turn to **70**. Go ahead, waiting won't do any good.

276

You run like crazy down the hall to discover that it ends in a spiral staircase. Now you hesitate – why? Ahh, you hear some sound from up the stairs. Sounds like rats to me. But if you think it sounds like footsteps – who am I to argue? Up the stairs you run, higher and higher, slower and slower, panting harder and harder. Not in too good shape, are you? I can see your point, you would much prefer it if I were running and you were doing the complaining. Point taken. Aha! A door, locked, but a few good bashes take care of that. You are through – and turn instantly to **95**.

277

Along the road, very lonely, not a soul in sight, wind keening through the branches of the leafless trees like the ghosts of drowned sailors. And ahead a deep chasm spanned by a long bridge.

Or rather it *used* to be spanned by this crummy second-rate bridge which has now collapsed in the middle. Yes, thank you for pointing it out: it is obvious to me, or to a retarded child for that matter, that your quarry did not come this way. About face and rush quickly to **290** to pick up his trail.

278

Well, what do you know! As the flame comes close and maniac laughter bellows out . . .

A trident flashes through the air! The brute's wrist is caught between the tines and pinned to the ground, the flame snuffed out. Oh, how he roars and swears, but before he can free himself a net falls and envelops him – while hordes of laughing sadists rush out and kick him and tie him up.

Sadists? Of course – they are the Sons of Sadism themselves. You are saved! And right behind them is Sadie the Sadistic herself who cuts your vines and frees you.

'**Did you get it? Tell me!**' she begs, and you point proudly to the tree branch where the Jewel of the Jungle safely hangs. Squealing shrilly, like any young sadist she pulls it down and spins in happy circles:

'**You have done it!**' she exults. '**And Sadie the Sadistic keeps her word. You shall have your reward.**'

I wonder what it will be? You wonder too. So let us stop this feckless wondering and find out at **147**.

279

Strong, isn't it! With one swipe of a paw, it tore the sword from your grasp and knocked you across the room. It has bounced away – but it will charge again. You are doomed, unless you would like to hear my advice now. You do? Good. While there is still time flip quickly to **326**.

280

You run! And I don't blame you. Crashing through the undergrowth, around the trees, up the hills and down the dales until you stream with sweat. You stagger into the shade of a large tree, panting for breath, turn and look –

And there is the hideous creature just behind you!

No chance to think. Nock arrow, draw bow – and shoot as it charges and its foul breath washes over you.

Zip now to **88** to see if you are still alive.

281

Through some miracle of millennia-vanished science this large room has clouds for a ceiling and is filled with a rushing wind and a driving rain. You quickly have enough of this. Hurrying, you discover that there is a door to the north to **300**, and another to the west to **210**. You leave.

282

Not too smart. You can't cut this net and he snares you with it and hurls you to the ground – and stands on your wrist with his big foot so you can't stab him with the sword. He waves his trident at the roaring crowd and speaks in the direction of the royal box:

'Tell me, oh mighty Sadie the Sadistic, do I kill this swine or do you wish me to spare its life? Thumbs up for life – thumbs down and I plunge my trident into its heart. Which shall it be?'

Which shall it be indeed! A very good question. You must use your APB to find out. You have just enough strength left to flip the coin. If it is heads go to **209**, if tails to **233**.

Not too smart. He cuts the net from your hand with his razor-sharp sword, beats you to the ground with his shield – and stands on your wrist with his big foot so you can't stab him with the trident. He waves his sword at the roaring crowd and speaks in the direction of the royal box as he cries out:

'Tell me, oh mighty Sadie the Sadistic, do I kill this swine – or do you wish me to spare its life? Thumbs up for life – thumbs down and I plunge my sword into its heart. Which shall it be?'

Which shall it be indeed! A very good question. You must use your APB to find out. You have just enough strength left to flip the coin. If it is heads go to **274**, if tails to **243**.

Don't be too depressed. So you missed two in a row. Instead of sobbing and feeling sorry for yourself be stern! That's better. Shoot another arrow – to **184** if it's heads, to **257** if tails.

The door closes behind you with a sickening thud – there is no way back. You can stop tearing at it with your fingernails now! That's it, stand tall, stand proud, accept your fate like a true Field Agent of the Special Corps. And

I heard that! Muttering insults about me, your only friend, won't help at all. Hark – footsteps approaching. Another brute in human form steps from the darkness. He has a shield on his right arm and waves a sword that he carries in his right hand. And there is a net over his left arm and he carries a trident-spear in that hand as well. He speaks . . .

'**Lowly worm, you are about to do battle in the arena for the greater glory of Sadie the Sadistic and her bank account – long may it grow! Choose your weapons now. If it is the trident and net you wish take them and proceed to 100. Or if you prefer the buckler and short sword go to 173. Now choose!**'

You've done it! Bullseye number three and you are the winner. Robbing Good, poor loser he, throws his bow to the ground and jumps up and down on it. Oh well, let him have his tantrum. You smile and watch and when he is done you tell him to pay up. He must do you the favour, the promised favour.

'**Yeah, yeah, I know, the favour. I even know what it is.**'

He knows what favour you want? Goodness, how can he know that? To discover what he knows flip now to **23**.

Running wasn't such a great idea since this porcuswine not only snorts and chuffs like a runaway locomotive – it runs just as fast as one. Hot on your heels it comes, nose lowered, eyes gleaming, quills rattling with frenzy. Right behind you – right on to you!

Ouch! That must have hurt. With a twist of its cruel

head it has hurled you right back to **260** to hopefully decide on a better course this time.

288

So who said that you can win them all. You missed, and he is creeping up on you. All you need is one more bullseye and you are home free. Aim and shoot, that's the way. Heads to **5**, tails to **133**.

289

You got another bullseye, while the scowling ruffian broke his arrow against a rock. He's not as good as he says he is. You have two now, hurrah! Quick, shoot another arrow. Heads is **288**, tails **166**.

290

Hurrying along you come out of a group of trees and see a man armed with a brass-bound club strolling towards you. My, you can move quickly when you want to. Off the road and into the copse and before he reaches you you have whisked out your knife and whittled yourself a stout walking staff. Very smart. Only I would get the knife out of sight as well.

As the evil-looking customer looms close you must make up your mind. If you ask him for information go to **132**. If you ignore him then to **154**.

291

Come on now, you can't be *that* stupid. Shift it to **201**.

292

If you answered that it is the displacement between two levels of hydrogen, which in the absence of radiative corrections would be zero due to the Coulomb degeneracy, score 1,356 points and go majestically to **229**. If you answered something with a different kind of degeneracy creep to **89**.

293

A lot of old rusty machines in here. You walk around them and find another exit to the north, to **295**, or you could go west to **269**.

294

Is that fresh air that you smell – or only an illusion generated by a millennia-old fresh air generator? Is it a fraud upon your senses? Who knows? You certainly don't. Better move on. A choice of two exits: **226** to the south – or **264** to the west.

295

Flickering and ghastly red light, most depressing. Hurry. The west opening goes to **244**, the south to **293**.

296

I don't blame you for feeling exhausted – but to stop now would be to court certain death. The millennia-dead scientists have done something to the air in this chamber that has rendered it as thick as molasses. You have to labour for minutes to draw in one breath of air and labour for what seems like hours to push your leg forward a single step against its resisting substance. But you are a battler, you are! It is hard but you have done it. You have discovered a way out to **247** to the east, and another to **226** to the west.

297

A long, rusty chamber filled with nameless objects, the floor covered with cold water through which you wade. It takes you some time to discover that this place has only two exits: to the west to **227**, or to the south to **211**.

298

Whether you answered the Battle of Hastings or not appears to make no difference and scores no points in this futile game because the Star Beast is sound asleep and snoring out clouds of smoke. You also note that Prof. Geisteskrank was only feigning sleep on his part and had really been working to open his cage and has done so and has already escaped through the door marked EXIT.

If you rush after him go to **35**. Or, if you proceed with trepidation, then go to **197**.

299

The dragon nods approval and speaks: 'You are far wiser, oh blood-filled mammal, than this idiot here who just screamed at me until I had to throw him into the cage. Now hear this. I am the Star Beast trapped here millennia ago by the evil Kakaloks. But they are all dead and good riddance. I could leave now but I kind of got to like the place after the first million years. I have colour TV, a good supply of coal, a big potty, so what the hell. I can also read minds. The professor wants to blow up the universe which, since I live in it, I am kind of against. While you want to bring him to justice which is OK by me. But you get him and get out of here only if you can answer my riddles. If you don't want to play I eat you right now. Ready?'

Some big choice! You nod with great reluctance. The great Star Beast riddle session begins:

'Answer quickly or you become breakfast. Who is buried in Grant's Tomb?'

If you think it is General Grant, go to **201**.

If you don't know, turn to **291**.

300

This stone-carved chamber is filled with a secret gas from a millennia-old source. It is laughing gas and you laugh and weep with joy and stagger in circles. Get a grip on yourself!

That's better. Between bellows of joy you determine that you can leave to the east to **217** or to the south to **281**. Cackling ferociously you go . . .

You climb . . . and you climb . . . and you climb – and eventually and reluctantly decide that this was not the galaxy's best idea. You are never going to make it to the top. After a rest you descend again with trembling limbs to **128**.

It worked – you are really fast on your feet. You jumped and the creature missed. But here it comes again and you have no choice but to jump again – this time jump to **331**.

Rattling rocketships! I can't believe it! It worked. The lord of the jungle has curled up at your feet and is licking your hand! You have reason to be proud. The crowd goes wild with applause because they have never seen anything like this before. That's it, take a bow, wipe the lion spit off on your shirt at the same time.

Smiling and bowing – and giving the lion a last friendly pat – you proceed wtih great dignity to **335**.

304

That's it, get into the chair, sit down – Perishing planets!
The seat has dropped open and you are falling, falling –
right down to **93**.

305

Rattling rocketships! I can't believe it! It worked. The lord
of the plains has curled up at your feet and is licking your
hand! You have reason to be proud. The crowd goes wild
with applause because they have never seen anything like
this before. That's it, take a bow, wipe the wolf spit off on
your shirt at the same time.

Smiling and bowing – and giving the wolf a last friendly
pat – you proceed with great dignity to **335**.

306

Darkness engulfs you as you slide down the slippery rock
tube, faster and faster – kind of fun, isn't it? Really, you
don't think it is fun? And there you go cursing again . . .
hark! Is that water we hear? It must be.

Still wrapped in stygian darkness you shoot through the
air. Take a deep breath, that's the way, and . . . SPLASH!
. . . you fall into the underground river. Very good, swim
up, you don't have much choice. Yes, you can suck in
some air now.

You are being carried downstream. About all you can do
is tread water and hope for the best. Yes, that is light
ahead. You are out in the sunshine now. Isn't that a
decrepit bridge we passed under? Looks familiar. So does

the shoreline. If you are tired that little beach would be a good spot to go ashore (turn to **3**) or you could land at those rocks by turning to **198**. If neither pleases you just hang in there until you are swept around a bend and can come ashore on a sandbar at **2**.

With a sudden lithe movement six tonnes of porcuswine leaps into the air, reverses neatly and lands facing in the opposite direction. You now find yourself facing the ham end of the porcuswine, not the world's most attractive sight either! Before you retreat the prickly porker calls back to you.

'Most people don't know it, but porcuswine have little curly tails just like pigs – without quills on them. You'll see my most attractive caudal appendage just before you. Grab on, kiddo, because here we go!'

You seize the tail in both hands – and just in time! With a roar and a grunt the porcuswine is off crashing through the forest. Branches, twigs, leaves, boulders – everything is tossed aside and flies by as he thunders along. Singing of course. This is a pretty revolting way to travel, and you have really had enough of it and are about to let go when the creature comes to a sliding halt. There is the sound of human screaming, a voice crying out in terror, and you run quickly past the acres of quills to see what it is all about at **309**.

What a sight! A line of robots walks up, walks by you – shouting and complaining and crying out. Really crying, too, oily tears running down their faces. And they have something to cry about because they are chained together by a chain that runs through a hole in every robot's head. You watch aghast, eyes bugging more than a bit, as they stagger on. Fifty of them at least. And behind them comes the robot slave master. A burly brute who holds the end of the chain in one hand, while he threatens them with a dangerous-looking gun in his other hand. Not only that but he has a whip made of barbed wire in his other hand with which he whips the robots so that they scream in metallic agony.

Don't be snide – of course I can count. And, yes, I can count to three. I know I said three hands. That is because he has three arms . . .

Watch out! While we were talking the vicious brute spotted you: he is raising the gun. Run, fight, do something!

Too late. Before you can do anything, he leers through the sights and fires at you point blank!

You will find out what happens to you at 324.

309

Wonderful! The evil Prof. Geisteskrank lies prone and helpless, being crushed into the mud by a giant hoof. He is armed, dangerous, ready to kill you. But can do nothing for the giant porcuswine has him trapped.

'This is it, old friend,' the porcuswine says. 'It is time for good chums to say goodbye. I know that you have a matter-transmitter in your pocket, and I also know that as soon as you touch this screaming nutcase I have put the blocks to good things will happen. I know you and he will matter-transmit the heck out of here. But before you go – let's have one last rendering of *The Pigish Chorus* from Der Meisterswiner.'

And this you do, with enthusiasm, for you owe a lot to

this old porker. You and he belt out the tune accompanied
by the background music of Geisteskrank's pained cries.

Then you are done and the porcuswine lifts its hoof. The
prof grabs for his gun, you grab for him and you press the
button . . .

To find out how this all comes out you will have to turn
at once to **338**.

310

Not too good! He jumps over your sword and leaps forward,
dagger swishing. You dodge – but not quickly enough.
The hilt catches you on the side of the helmet, stunning
you, you fall – fall all the way to **79**.

311

The coast is clear. Just jungle outside with a path running
close by. You step out carefully, then walk boldly down
the path. Proud of yourself, aren't you? Yes, you did all
right – if you forget about putting the Roc to sleep. Right,
accidents do happen.

You make good time for the path is smooth and straight.
While you walk you plan ahead. Bring the Jewel of the
Jungle to Sadie the Sadistic. Find out from her where Prof.
Geisteskrank is hiding. Grab the old nutter – then back
you go. Not bad. I hope it works that smoothly. I'm
getting as fed up with this planet as you are.

Yes, not *as* fed up because I can't feel all the bug bites
and the knocks on the head. Agreed . . .

You stop when you hear the loud clanking and screeching
coming from the trail ahead. And it is coming towards you.
It doesn't sound too good.

If you stand strong and face up to what is coming march sternly to **325**.

Or if you feel discretion is the better part of valour, dive into hiding in the jungle at **308**.

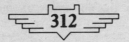

How was I to know that it was a dumb idea? It was your decision after all. You have pressed the button on your invisibility belt and have used up a second charge. Only one left! And it was a complete waste. It is common knowledge that porcuswine can't see very well with their little red eyes. But they do smell pretty good with their little red noses. (And I agree, they do smell pretty bad to *your* little red nose.)

The great beast came tearing along, instantly smelled your presence and with a twist of its great head hurled you into the air and right back to **260** again – to hopefully, consider a wiser and less dangerous course of action this time.

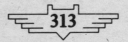

Wow – this is really a bummer! Straight uphill with scarcely a foothold. You pull yourself from bunch to bunch of grass, just able to grab them for a handhold. Sweat pours from you in streams, filling your boots until they slop over.

You stop to rest – but must go on before you weaken. Yet the end is in sight, the crest of the ridge above. With your last energy, you drag yourself up and creep over the top to **245**.

314

This is hard work. The big green fruit are each about the size of a grapefruit, only the wrong colour of course. They are high in the trees and you have to climb up to get them. Each one is attached by a tough stem that will not break. You try cutting one off with your sword – and it works fine.

Except the fruit plunges to the ground and explodes with a juicy splosh. Be more careful next time. Hold the stem, then cut it – that's it. Then climb carefully down and place the fruit on the ground. And climb the tree for more.

Time passes slowly until you have all that you can carry on the ground. With a bit of vine you tie all their stems together, get the green bundle over your shoulder – and stagger fruitily to **113**.

315

Whistling happily and twanging your bowstring as you go, you go. Down the broken-bone road, kicking a skull along in front of you just for fun. This world has done you no good, no good at all! You are becoming as hardened as the most hardened criminal around.

Sadie was right – after less than a day's walk you see the decayed roofs of a town over the next hill and beside the road a sign which reads:

ENDSVILLE – POPULATION 467 AND DECREASING RAPIDLY

As you read the sign you hear a scream of pain ending with a mortal gurgle: and the sign clicks and the number now reads 466. This is a really tough place. But you must go on!

You start towards town – then stop as you hear heavy breathing and cursing coming towards you around the bend. Where there is heavy breathing and cursing there is usually someone doing the HB and C you reason. You will face up to the danger – no turning back now!

You nock an arrow to your bow and wait expectantly for **116** to appear.

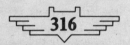

316

You are the winner! On bended knees the rusty robotic loser pleads for mercy.

'**Oh mighty stranger – you have vanquished me. It would take but a swing of your mighty sword to polish me off and send my metallic body plummeting into the gorge behind me. But mercy, I beg! I am a paid-up member of the Robotic Guards Union and I retire next year on half pay. Let me but survive and I will tell you how to avoid the pitfalls on the far side of this chasm. Will you do that?'**

Being a real sweety-pie at heart you nod and beam and go to **78**. Or are you going to be strong and make sure this tricky mechanical monster doesn't pull any fast ones behind your back? If so thinking of gloom and death you step forward to **77**.

317

After much shouting, and a few kicks in the can, you get the robots sorted out and marching in the right direction. In the lead is a robot who swears he knows where to find Sadie the Sadistic. You hope so, too, since you have heard more than enough robotic belly-aching. You wonder who made these metallic mothers – and just why.

The march continues through the afternoon and the robot pilot swears that you are getting close to Sadie's hangout. You hope he is right for your feet are getting tired and the Jewel of the Jungle is beginning to scratch where you have it hidden inside your clothes.

Sudden shouting and robotic panic. Their ranks open up and you see a hairy giant armed with a club on the path ahead. The creature speaks:

'Arrghh! I'm stealing your robots buddy – and don't try to stop me! I'm going to work them to death in my cat pudding factory where we make the best kind of dog food!'

Decisions, decisions. Should you help these robots? They mean nothing to you. Or let them go off to a lifetime of labour in the canine gourmet works?

It is up to you. If you wish to fight for robotic rights, go righteously to 157.

However if you wish to leave them to the fate they richly deserve stroll casually to 268.

318

What a sight! Blue sky above, red-stained yellow sand below. Are the red stains blood? I couldn't say, best not to think about it. Listen to the roar of the crowd. I wonder what they are so excited about? Oh, yes, I see now, a great wolf has just entered the arena through a little door. It howls and yawns, looks about – and sees you. It seems to be smiling. Or maybe it is just showing you its fangs. And, yes, it is coming this way. You raise the feather, not really the best weapon.

It stands before you and howls again, its breath washes over you in a fetid wave, it approaches . . .

If you feel that tickling it with the feather will make it laugh and not eat you why go to 152.

If jumping aside when it leaps seems preferable, go to **183**.

319

Time to think again, if you don't mind. All you have is one crummy sword with dents in it – against all those thugs in Endsville. Not too good. See if you can promote something a bit more deadly from Sadie at **41**.

320

Nothing good. Your blow misses and the robot catches you with a counter-blow. Felling you. Rattling with rage the thing attacks – but you lash out with your legs. Lash all the way to **316**.

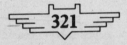

321

You dive through the door and slam it shut behind you – and just in time for there is a crunching roar as the tower falls in. The door shakes and bounces as the stones from above crash against it. You hear a terrible sound behind you – you turn and see . . .

Yipes! It is a giant tiglon sharpening its claws on the rock wall. It hears you and wheels about and roars again – look at those teeth!

You raise your sword as it attacks. What a puny defence against a creature this size. One of its teeth is longer than the sword. I have an idea . . .

Oh, you don't want to hear my idea. All right then, stand and fight at **279**, I don't care.

But if you would like a bit of sage advice, turn at once to 326.

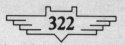

You open the door and step aside. Tonnes of thundering rocks rumble in and bury the tiglon. Only its tail protrudes from the mountain of rubble. This twitches once and is still. What a killer you are! Swaggering you slip your sword back into the scabbard, stroll across the chamber – then open the door there and step through to 188.

What fear possesses you! I can feel your entire body a-tremble as the great crashing comes closer. Trees fall and bushes are uprooted as into the clearing comes . . .

A giant porcuswine. It fixes you with one beady eye and speaks.

'You know, kiddo, you have a capacity for getting into trouble that far surpasses that of any human being I have ever met. I have been watching with stunned amazement your recent adventure in mutual trust and how all the other squishy human beings betrayed you. It makes the so-called lower beasts look good! I have something important to tell you – but before I do you must choose . . . and choose well. We are going to sing a song, and if you choose the correct song very good things will happen to you. Choose the wrong song and death will fly mighty close and seize you in its talons.

'Now – what's your choice? Do you want to sing *Rest in the Bosom of the Sty* or *Swing Low, Sweet Porcuswine*?'

Boy, some choice. This is too important a decision to be

left to chance – or science – so no coin-flipping this time. You will have to decide by yourself. If it is going to be the one about the sty, go to **68**. Or if you think you have a far better chance by living with *Swing Low* then go a-trembling to **52**.

You've been hit! You cry out!

More in shock than in pain – because you have been drenched. The gun is an immense water-pistol and you have been splashed!

The brute realizes his mistake. The water-pistol is for the robots. If he shoots them with it, they will rust and fall and suffer the hideous fate of turning to junk.

The robot-slaver drops the gun and reaches for his sword. But too late! Roaring with sodden rage, you are upon him, hacking the hangers on his scabbard so it drops to the ground. Hacking his suspenders so his trousers drop to the ground as well. Pinking him in the derrière with your swordtip so he howls and flees. Holding up his trousers as he goes. A wonderful sight.

The robots seem to think so too. They flock around you and pat you on the back and say nice things about you – while you pull the chains out through the holes in their heads and free them. A large robot steps forward and kneels before you, seizes up your hand and kisses it getting it all oily:

'Oh good master, you have saved us,' the thing declaims in a decidedly tinny voice. 'We had given up all hope until this moment. You see we are the property of the Duke of Groann who was an evil master. He beat us and gave us cheap oil and let our batteries run down and bought secondhand spares. Then complained that we were doing second-rate work. Look at the scratches here where he whipped me. Ohh, it was so awful we could not take it any more!'

He is interrupted by a small robot with six arms. It flails its arms about like an intoxicated windmill while it talks.

'The Duke is a monster! He humiliated and beat us until we cried, then he laughed at our misery. So we had to escape him. We ran away but we were caught and condemned to death and we were being marched to the lake and were to be pushed in and rust away forever!'

At this thought all the robots begin to wail and cry and fall about. They really are a disgusting bunch of whiners and you wonder why the Duke didn't junk them years ago. They group around you and splatter you with oil and it is time to decide.

Do you want to carry on with this metallic junkyard? They may be wimps but they are still robots and you could get some mileage out of them. If you decide to enlist their aid lead them to **317**.

Or if you want to go it alone, then go it on **151**.

325

Louder and louder, more and more horrible. Now that you mention it I do think that your knees are shaking a bit. I'm *sure* that it is not fear. Just fatigue. Why don't you take a rest – sitting down in the jungle where you can peek out from safety at whatever is coming down the pike? That's it, slip silently into hiding at **308**.

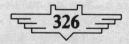

326

You can't fight that thing – so use brains instead of brawn. Rush over to the door by which you entered, that's it.

Stand there . . . wait for it . . . grab the handle. The tiglon charges . . . NOW! Turn to **322!**

That's it – pull on the thing's neck – harder! It's turning, heading for the tower – but too low! It's going to crash . . .

Wow! This Roc of Ages must have subconscious sonar. Even when it's asleep it doesn't crash. With a single flap it lifted up and settled on the top of the tower in a perfect belly-landing.

What's that sound? Either the thing is snoring or grumbling. Don't hang around to find out. Slip down on to the top of the tower, draw your sword – not a bad idea, since you don't know if this is the correct tower that leads to the Jewel – or the one that leads to certain death. About time you found out – head for the trapdoor. It creaks when it opens and a puff of dank gas comes out. No, it doesn't look too nice down there . . .

'**Stop, you poisoning pismire! You'll not escape a horrible lingering death that easily!**'

Yes, the Roc is awake and in quite a temper! Beak clashing, claws tearing grooves in the solid rock of the tower!

Say, you can really move fast when you want to! Through the trapdoor, bolt it behind you and down the steps two at a time. That kingsize sparrow is really annoyed. You can still hear him roaring and scratching, the whole tower is shaking. He'll have it down in a minute! Jump three steps at a time – why not! Rocks breaking loose, cracks in the wall – but there is the bottom and a door ahead.

Roaring and crashing? Now that you mention it I do hear something awful coming from the door. But I also know that the tower is falling in. Better the devil you don't know than the devil you do. Sword ready – jump!

Right to **231**.

328

Don't be too downhearted, you can't win them all. Yes, I understand, it's not *all* that you are worried about – you would just like to win one once in a while. All right, no point in crying over spilt milk. Time to put the old thinking cap on and count your assets. Very few, aren't they? You still have the matter-transmitter, but you can't use that until you have the prof by the hand. No swords, no weapons, your clothing is torn and there is a hole in the sole of your right shoe. Yes, I *do* feel sorry for you, but that is not going to get you very far. And your left foot hurts. Do you remember why – very smart of you to remember! – so turn at once to **11**.

If you don't remember and your brain needs jogging a bit, take a look at **56**.

329

Crunch! The snake contracts and everything goes black. When it slithers away you can only lie, half-stunned, as the serpent-master steals everything that you have. The rest of your smokebombs, your sword – then he roots through your pockets for the rest. The matter-transmitter doesn't interest him, but he takes everything else that you have. Including the seven gold coins.

And when he is all done, just to add insult to injury, he hisses out quick orders and the snake is upon you again, wrapping you and dragging you to the edge of the nearby cliff – and hurling you over!

But you are not dead yet! You clutch at the roots that project from the cliff, hanging on for dear life, and only when the snake and snake-master have gone do you pull yourself back up with the last of your energy, right to 328.

330

'A wise choice,' the Duke of Groann says, swinging you up on the horse behind him and galloping off with you. Down the road you go with the angry cries of the others ringing in your ears. Goodness – what names they are calling you! But you care not – for this caper is almost over. Onward and onward the great horse gallops until you come to a grassy glade by the banks of a stream. The Duke stops, dismounts and helps you down.

'And now the truth,' he says, and you do not like the look of his evil grin. You turn to flee but too late – he pulls out his sword, knocks you to the ground with the hilt, then puts the point to your throat.

'Heh, heh!' he chortles. 'Fooled you – didn't I? If you want to know the truth I am bankrupt, bust. The bank took my castle away, I got this nag from Rent-a-Horse and am behind with the payments, my armour is rusty and even the gilt on my codpiece is really brass. But you shall restore my fortunes. Where are the gold coins hidden? Speak or I lean on the sword and you have snuffed it.'

No, you don't have much choice. The point of the sword sinks into your throat and you cry out where the coins have been hidden. The Duke chortles with joy, cuts your belt with his sword – then gallops away in a great cloud of dust.

Is this the end? It sure looks like it. You cough at the dust, seize your waistband, count your assets – which are zero – and contemplate the future.

Nothing. All your weapons gone, now the gold, the

matter transmitter won't work without the prof being present. You are doomed forever to this rotten prison planet . . .

Hist! Listen to me and stop feeling sorry for yourself for one moment. Now tie a knot in the belt so you don't lose your trousers and pay close heed. There is one thing I haven't told you about yet. I was saving it for the right moment and this looks like the moment. While you were under hypnosis – you didn't know we had you hypnotized did you? The Special Corps does not reveal all its secrets! Anyway, while you were hypnotized, we planted a miniature time machine in the joint of your right index finger. All you have to do is crack your knuckle to energize it. That's it, don't feel foolish, pull hard on your finger. As soon as it goes crack you will go to **80**.

331

The creature missed again. I agree, it is a little clumsy, but all it needs is one crunch of those mighty jaws and you have had it.

You are going to do *what?* Stare it down? Prove that human beings can master the creatures of the forest with steely gaze and power of will? That is really a crazy – I mean *great* idea! Good luck – for here it comes again. Raging and tearing up the sand, teeth gleaming in the fitful sunshine, closer and closer . . .

You stand your ground, fixing it with your firm gaze and, still standing and staring, proceed to **303**.

332

Yes, I agree, tickling wasn't the world's greatest idea. The great ugly creature simply brushed you aside but at least it didn't bite you or maul you. And here it comes again!

You jump aside so that it misses you and jump right to **331**.

333

At least that is behind you! Scramble into the tunnel and take ten. That's it, breathe deeply. This alien artefact is dangerous enough – I only hope that the professor was as fast on his feet as you are. Rested? Right, carry on, not much choice here. Straight on down the tunnel.

Why are you stopping? I see now, the tunnel ends ahead. Slowly and carefully now, peering out with extreme caution . . .

Looks clear enough. But counting on past experience you can't trust a thing in this ancient prison built by the long dead Kakaloks.

An empty room, a single exit and a pointing arrow with a sign: *AL LA STELBESTO*. That's simple enough – to the Star Beast. Imprisoned here millions of years ago. Should be safe enough with the beast long dead . . .

Yes, I heard it too. It *did* sound just a bit like a giant bestial roar. Probably just the ground settling. Don't think about it. About all you can do is – shoulders back – walk proud, into the tunnel to **19**.

What a walk! A hot day, a rough road, the ropes on your wrists chafe and hurt. Really rough. The thug who is tied to you in front pulls on the rope, the mug behind walks on your heels. This is really bad. So don't swear at me! I didn't get you into this fix – and I know that my suffering is at a long distance. Yes, I *do* sympathize with you. I'll punch your TS card anytime. But look – the little parade is stopping! You drop by the roadside with the others and hark! – the rough-looking type who is tied to the rope in front of you is talking.

'**I hope you have prayed your last prayer to whatever disgusting gods you pray to, because your life is soon to end, filthy-one.**'

Filthy-one – he's some example to talk! Pot and the kettle and so forth. But you're right, ignore the insults and query him as to just what the hell he is talking about.

'**I am talking about the Arena of Sadie the Sadistic from whence no man emerges alive. You been under a rock or something all of your life that you never heard of Sadie? Ohh, you just arrived on the planet. Bad luck. What did you do to get sent to this dump of a prison planet? Oh, multiple murders with an atomic chainsaw . . .**'

Well done, a little white lie always works wonders. See how he moves away uneasily. You have taught him a bit of respect. Now, when he resumes talking there is a more humble tone to his voice.

'**Well you see, sir, Sadie the Sadistic is a real mean one. She is head of this gang, the Sons of Sadism, that rules this entire area with fear and violence. She rules them with an iron fist and spiked boots. Oh, they walk in fear of her they do, spike marks all over their backs. We** *all* do. In order to keep her terrible ruffians happy she entertains them with beer and circuses. Nobbled that bit from the Old Romans, only changed bread for beer. Kept the Arena though, and the Games – and that's where we are going now!'

Even as your new friend finishes speaking he is kicked to his feet – while you jump to yours before the boot arrives. On you march and onward, until at last a gloomy building appears ahead. Through the gaping portal your band of slaves goes, into a cavernous room lit by the flickering light of flame-worms. The portal slams shut behind you and your bonds are cut away. But there can be no escape for your little mob is surrounded by heavily armed guards. A sneering fat swine of a slave-trainer mounts an empty barrel and speaks:

'Silence oh you slaves who are lower than a snake's belly. Silence! Let it be known that you are here to serve our gracious leader, fine woman that she is!, Sadie the Sadistic.'

At the mention of this name a chorus of groans goes up from the captives and you groan along with the rest – then yipe like the rest when the slavers lash out with their whips.

'Silence swine! You are here to fight in the arena and will undoubtedly die there. Ninety-nine point nine nine nine of you slaves do snuff it in there. But die happy – for you have served a noble cause! Now you will choose how you will enter the arena. Go – and I mean quickly! – through that door to 273!'

335

You have returned to the room with the four doors having survived the perils of one door you won't try the same door again. So choose between the others. You will remember door one takes you to **285**, door two to **239**, or door three to **251**, while door four will take you to **102** – but you can only enter this door if you have been to the arena two times and have survived your two trips there. Choose!

336

Now look here, recruit. If you fall into that water with all this armour on you will go to the bottom and stay there. Not only will you die from drowning but you will never become an agent in the Special Corps. Rarely in life do we have the opportunity to have a second chance. You now have a second chance. Proceed shamefully to **271**.

337

Take no chances, that's the way. Crawl by the chair and down the tunnel and . . .

They thought of this one too. A trapdoor opens beneath your feet and, scrabble as hard as you can with broken fingernails against the unyielding walls, you fall down and down to **93**.

338

CONGRATULATIONS!

You have done it! You have succeeded where all others have failed! You have captured the professor and brought him safely back to the secret headquarters of the Special Corps.

His curses as he is led away by the guards are as sweet music to your ears. But enough – the time has come!

Step forward proudly while I pin on the wings of a Full Field Agent of the Special Corps!

Blush with pride and hold your head high as you go forth into the world a changed human being. No longer a weak and foolish citizen who sings with porcuswine.

You have done it! You have won.

THE END